I0675675

THEIR PURPLE GIRL

DAISY EMORY

TURBO KITTEN

Their Purple Girl by Daisy Emory.

Copyright © 2020 Turbo Kitten Industries. All rights reserved.

Cover design by Temptation Creations.
Interior design by Turbo Kitten Industries™.
Published by Turbo Kitten Industries™.

Without limiting the rights under the copyright reserved above, no part of this publication may be reproduced, stored in or introduced into a retrieval system, or transmitted in any form or by any means (electronic, mechanical, by photocopying, recording or otherwise) without the prior written permission of the copyright owner and the publisher of the book.

 The scanning, uploading, and distribution of this book via the Internet or by any other means without the permission of the author is illegal and punishable by law. Please purchase only authorized printed or electronic editions and do not participate in or encourage electronic piracy of copyrighted materials. Your support of the author's rights is appreciated.

This is a work of fiction. Names, characters, places and incidents either are the product of the author's imagination or are used fictitiously. Any resemblance to actual persons, living or dead, events, or locales is entirely coincidental.

To Cassie and Ericka: You two keep me writing on my darkest author days. Thank you.

CHAPTER ONE

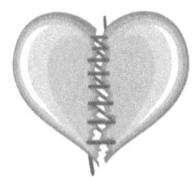

"Cameron, why is your hair purple?" Mother shouted from my doorway when she recovered enough from having her mouth agape.

I twirled a chunk of my gloriously purple hair around my finger and smiled. "Isn't it gorgeous?"

"N-No, it is not gorgeous! You c-cannot have p-purple hair," she stammered.

"I read the school rules four times, and they have no rules against dying your hair," I informed her and flipped the hair over my shoulder.

"Do you have any i-idea what the people at church are going to think when they see my daughter with p-p-purple hair?" She fanned her face and leaned heavily against the doorframe like it was the only thing holding her up.

I rolled my eyes at my overly dramatic mother. "You can tell the prudes that you love your daughter and love her individuality."

"You look like a...a..."

"Heathen?" I supplied, already knowing where this was headed.

"Yes!" she screeched and then began reciting her favorite bible verses.

I heaved a deep sigh, walked to her, and set my hands on her shoulders. "It's not permanent dye, Mother. It will be gone within a couple of weeks. Just tell them what a horrible daughter I am and beg them to assist you in praying for my soul." She loved when people threw her a pity party, and I had just handed her one she could milk for the entire school year.

"Why did you have to do this when we just moved? This was supposed to be a fresh start," she whispered.

"It is a fresh start," I whispered. "For me, remember?"

She cringed and nodded. "You're right. Enjoy your purple hair while you have it. And Cameron, try to have fun and make friends, okay? Not everyone is a terrible person."

I gave her a tight smile. "Right."

She hesitated a second and then turned. "Don't be late for your first day of school."

"Yes, Mother," I called after her as cheerily as I could.

She turned around, rolled her eyes at me, and then hurried down the stairs. Probably to go call one of her church gossipers to get the jump on the rumors of my hair before they started spreading.

Now that she had checked on me, I could do my makeup and leave without her commenting on how much eyeliner or eyeshadow I used. According to her, more than a thin layer made me look like a streetwalker.

One would think she had grown up here in the South instead of in Northern California.

Thinking of my old home made me both homesick and just sick. I squashed the memories down, grabbed my backpack, and ran down the stairs.

"Bye, Mom! See you tonight!" I yelled just before slamming the front door closed behind me.

It was best if I didn't even give her a chance to say anything to me before I left.

Once outside of our cute little two-story cottage, I shrugged my backpack's shoulder straps up higher and headed towards the city of Sheldon.

Well, what you called a city down here. It was maybe ten stores and three city buildings, plus the three school buildings.

It was so different from the huge town we had come from.

Yet, also cute and quaint.

We moved in a few weeks ago, but I refused to explore the town. I didn't want to explore all ten miles of it too quickly.

Okay, maybe I was being a little harsh.

"Hey, new girl," a deep female voice called.

I turned and nodded at my next door neighbor, Tamara. She had gorgeous dark skin and curly hair.

"Hey, neighbor," I called out.

She jogged across the street and walked beside me. "Excited for your first day of school?"

I scoffed. "Not at all. I'd rather just sit in the house and listen to music."

She reached out and touched a strand of my hair. "I like the color. It suits you."

"Thanks," I said and smiled at her. "So, what's this school like?"

She and I hadn't talked much, but girls were girls and as long as she wasn't a bitch, I would get along with her fine.

She shrugged. "Small town. Mostly caucasian, but there is about thirty percent Mexican population."

"Mexican or Latino?" I asked.

She arched a brow. "You know the difference?"

I smirked. "I grew up in California."

Her eyes widened. "No shit?"

I nodded.

"Well, I need to apologize then. I thought you were just another backwoods chick who I was going to have to teach what words are appropriate to call me and what aren't."

I arched a brow at her. "That bad here?"

She laughed. "Sometimes, but mostly that's the older people. Many of the younger generation are a bit more politically correct thanks to BookFace."

Mom had banned me from BookFace once the threats had started. "Right. So, are there any cute guys at this high school?"

She chuckled. "Girl, they know how to grow them down here. If you know what I mean?"

I laughed with her, and we finished our walk in companionable silence.

Maybe this first day of school wouldn't be so bad.

No sooner had I thought that than a guy slammed into my side, knocking me into Tamara, and knocking us all to the ground on the sidewalk.

"Oh, man. I'm so sorry," the guy said as he untangled himself from us.

Tamara and I helped each other up and I turned to yell at the guy, but my tongue stuck to the roof of my mouth as I took him in.

Muscled, tattooed, and hot as sin.

"Uh, are you okay?" I asked.

He smiled and brushed invisible dirt off my shoulder. "I am. Sorry for knocking you girls down. You okay, Tamara?"

She smiled at him. "I'm good, Sean. Busy day in the shop?"

Sean nodded and looked down at me. "Sorry I didn't catch your name."

I held out my hand. "I'm Cameron."

He shook my hand. "Nice to meet you. Sorry we met this way, but I really need to get moving. Work is busy today."

"We have to get to class, too. Bye, Sean." Tamara grabbed my arm and dragged me away from Sean. "Girl, close your mouth and wipe your drool."

I wiped my mouth, but it was dry, so I glared at her. "Whatever."

She laughed and shook her head. "You are hopeless! You won't survive meeting the Gods if you can't survive meeting Sean."

"The Gods?" I asked incredulously.

She nodded. "For the white girls at least. Three boys who they can't stop fawning over. The Gods of our stupid little school."

"Sounds interesting," I whispered.

She scoffed. "Hardly."

"You're holding out on me so I have to wait and see, aren't you?" I asked with narrowed eyes.

She smirked. "Maybe."

"I bet they're hideous, and you're just calling them that to get my hopes up. That's really rude, you know that?"

She laughed, but didn't deny it.

Wonderful.

We finally made it to the school, and as I had expected, there was very little racial diversity.

"You seem sad," Tamara commented.

"I really was hoping for more diversity."

She snorted. "Welcome to the south, girl."

"Where do I need to go to get my schedule?" I asked.

"Everyone goes to the football field to get their schedule," she explained. "Follow me."

I obeyed, looking around at the other kids, the majority of whom seemed younger than us. Most gave me weird stares, which I expected. Small towns would identify the new people immediately.

"Cool hair," a young girl whispered to me as she walked by, clutching her backpack to her chest.

"Thanks," I said back, smiling brightly, but she was already gone, giggling with her group of friends.

"Just remember that you won't be stuck here forever," Tamara whispered. "It's the only thing that helps me sleep at night."

I exhaled through my nose. "Right."

At the football field there were four lines, separated by last name. I waved to Tamara as we separated to our respective lines.

In front of me, three pretty girls in the latest fashion trend whispered together and giggled in high-pitched voices.

It surprised me to see such trendy clothes in this town.

"Did you use flavored juice packets to dye your hair?" one of the girls asked as they all turned around to look at me.

I pretended not to hear them, then looked up at them. "What?"

"Your hair—"

"Oh, I used a dye I bought while I was in California," I said, a bit louder than I needed to.

"California?" one of the girls asked with wide eyes and an open mouth.

"Yes, that's where I am from," I said with a nod.

"Why are you here then?" the prettiest of the girls asked with folded arms.

I shrugged. "My mother wanted a change of scenery."

"How sad for you," she said with a smirk and a hand on her hip.

Wonderful, my first enemy.

I pulled my cell phone out of my back pocket and sent a text to Tamara that read: *Trendy hicks are irritating.*

Her laugh carried over from the line she was in two over from me.

"So, the weirdo made a friend with the outcast already? Cute," the pretty girl said with a sneer.

"Look, Karen, you may be pretty, but that's all you will ever have. There are millions of girls prettier than you where I came from. Don't try to test me if you don't want to settle it with our fists. You can't handle it, trust me. So, turn around and leave me the fuck alone."

Her friends gasped while she flipped her hair and turned around with a harrumph.

Finally, I got my schedule and met back up with Tamara. We had all of the same classes together.

"How lucky is that?" I asked.

She laughed. "Girl, there are two hundred of us in the same grade. It's not that lucky. It's just what happens when there are so few of us and so few classes available."

"Whatever. Let's head to first period," I said and shoved my schedule in my back pocket.

"Had a little run in with the Queen?" she asked in a hushed whisper.

I rolled my eyes. "Sure. If that's what you call that average ass Karen."

She laughed so hard she ended up holding her stomach. "Oh, my god. Call her that to her face, I dare you."

"I already called her Karen."

Her mouth dropped. "You didn't?"

"Why would I lie about that?" I asked her.

"Well, don't get too much on her bad side. As much as I hate that wench, she rules this school and can turn them all against you. Trust me, that is not what you want to happen in this small town," she whispered.

I sighed and nodded. "Noted."

I hated to think there was one person who had so much power, but in a school that was so small, it did make sense. The guys would want to date her, the girls would want to be her or be her friend, and people like me would just be outliers.

I didn't want to make waves, but I did not want to be a pushover either. I didn't want what happened at my last school to happen here, too.

How did I ensure that I was safe, but not a pariah?

Was it such a thin line?

"Hey," Tamara whispered and set a hand on my shoulder.

I yelped and jumped back, eyes wide and breath panting.

She lowered her hand and tilted her head. "You okay?"

I nodded and took a deep breath. "Sorry, I spaced out for a minute. Yeah. I'm okay. What's up?"

She opened a door. "We're here. First period."

I nodded and walked in. I would have to figure everything out as I went along and hoped nothing horrible happened.

Not like my previous life.

"Sit next to me," Tamara whispered. "Please?"

She didn't even need to ask me, but I nodded and while she sat in the seat the farthest to the left, I sat beside her.

I did not expect someone to sit right beside me within two minutes.

Or for the person to be hot as Hades.

"Hey," he said and smiled at me. "This seat taken?"

I shrugged. "Probably not. It's a free town from what I've been told."

He leaned back and immediately people flocked to him, surrounding us.

Had I not been used to so many people being in one place, I would have felt claustrophobic.

"Girl, do you know who that is?" Tamara asked.

I turned and gave her my best irritated look.

"He's ones of the Gods."

I looked back at the sexy guy and then turned to her. "He is hot."

She exhaled. "Duh."

"So, new girl, what's your name?" the guy asked me once the others left to take their seats when the teacher walked in.

The teacher was a woman in her seventies, who wrote with chalk on a green chalkboard. I didn't even know those still existed. And her name was seriously Mrs. Twinkerton.

"Uh, I'm Cameron."

He held out his hand. "Branson. Nice to meet you."

We shook hands, and I enjoyed the warmth of his much larger hand around mine until he stopped and pulled his hand back.

The teacher went over the normal basic information about how the class would go, but I barely paid attention.

What was the likelihood that I could snag this hottie for myself?

There was no doubt that the girl from earlier had her eyes on him, but I wanted him, too. What steps could I take? Did I even want to get involved with the popular crowd?

Maybe it would be better to just stay in the background, as an outcast.

"Sign the syllabus and pass it back up," Mrs. Twinkerton instructed.

I signed, and Branson took my syllabus, adding it to the stack before passing it up towards the front.

We packed up our things and left, funneling out of the room.

"God number one has been met," Tamara whispered in my ear. "Now, let's see who you meet in class number two."

"Hopefully, they'll be just as hot as him," I whispered, and we giggled together.

"What are you giggling about?" Branson asked, walking behind us.

"Nothing, Branson. Just talking about our small town with California Girl here," Tamara answered.

"Must be a huge change going from a big city to this small-town dump," he commented.

"It's not a dump," I argued. "It's quaint and cute."

He rolled his eyes. "Right."

"It is cute," I said. "There's not gang violence, shootings, sheriff helicopters flying around at night searching for people running from them. No one hopping your fence at three in the morning to try to hide from cops. No fireworks going off at all hours of the night for three weeks around a holiday. It's quiet and cheerful. It's clean and well taken care of. It's...cute."

"Give it a few years and we'll see how you think then," he muttered.

I scoffed. "I don't plan on being here more than a couple of months past my eighteenth birthday."

"When is that?" Tamara asked.

"Three hundred and forty-five days," I answered.

Both looked at me with wide eyes.

I chuckled nervously. "Not that I'm counting." July 31st was going to be the day I escaped it all. My mother. Her religion. The oppression. Everything!

"Right," he said and smiled.

"Where are you going to go once you hit that date?" Tamara asked.

"Back to California, but to a smaller town in the north."

"You like small towns?" Branson asked.

"Some of them," I answered softly.

"Well, maybe you'll end up liking this town and won't leave," Tamara suggested.

At that, all three of us laughed loudly.

"Hey, Branson," the pretty girl from before called.

He sighed so softly that I wondered if I'd imagined it. "Hey, Sylvia."

She hooked her arm through his and pulled him ahead of Tamara and I. "You weren't talking to the trash, were you? Of course not. So, this weekend I was thinking we could catch a movie and then go watch the stars."

"Sounds boring," Tamara whispered to me.

I laughed and then covered it up by coughing into my hand when Sylvia turned to glare at us.

"I have plans with the guys this weekend," Branson said. "Sorry."

She pouted. "You said that last weekend, though."

"Probably will say it next, as well," I whispered to Tamara who had a coughing fit.

"Well, I'll talk to you later," he said, extricated himself from her hold and walked into the nearest classroom.

"Bye, Sylvia," Tamara said, waved, and pushed me into the classroom after Branson where had disappeared.

CHAPTER TWO

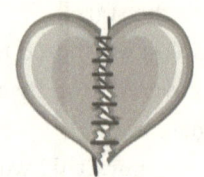

Second period was as boring as first, but there were two hot guys in this class. Luckily, they sat together so I didn't have to spend my time looking back and forth across the room at them.

Branson and the guy whispered together throughout class, and I did my best to ignore them.

But they were so hot.

Like, even California boy hot. How did they grow them like that here in the south?

"Stop drooling," Tamara whispered.

This time I didn't fall for her teasing and just glared at her, which made her laugh.

"So, what's their deal?" I asked in a whisper as we packed up our stuff. "Crazy? On and off again with Karen? Can't keep their hot dogs in their jeans?"

She let out a bark of laughter at my last question and quickly covered her mouth. "Oh, my God, girl. You are going to kill me. No, the Gods don't date Sylvia or her cronies. She wishes, but they just tolerate her presence because their parents force them to."

"Church?" I guessed.

She nodded.

Wonderful.

"So, they're single?" I asked.

She draped her arm around my shoulders and steered me out of the classroom. "Girl, you should steer clear of the Gods. Just find a simple southern boy you can push around. That's ninety percent of the population here."

"I like a challenge," I said with a shrug. "Why are they single?"

She shrugged and dropped her arm to pull her backpack up higher on her shoulders. "Honestly, no one knows. They could date any girl here that they want, but they don't. Or at least, no one confesses to having dated them for even a brief period of time."

"Are they gay and just don't want to admit it because...you know...south?" I asked.

She shrugged. "Your guess is as good as mine."

Well, that did set my plans a bit to the wayside.

Now that I was stuck in this southern town, I wanted to try and find some guys to make my few months here at least enjoyable.

Maybe I would just have to focus on that guy we ran into before school.

He had tattoos, and I was a sucker for tattoos.

"What are you smirking about?" Tamara asked.

"So, Karen and her cronies are single, too?" I asked. Normally, that type of girl was always in a relationship or at least on and off again with a relationship.

"Yep. They say they are holding out for the Gods, but the Gods don't want them. So, it's basically a ridiculous standoff."

I scoffed. "That *is* ridiculous. No guy is worth holding out for."

She eyed me sideways. "So, guess that means you aren't still holding out on that V card?"

I exhaled through my nose. "Uh, no. That ship sailed years ago. But don't you dare tell my mama."

She held her hands up and said, "I won't tell her anything."

"Good," I grumbled. "She wants to know everything with me, but she really doesn't. She would have a heart attack if she learned everything that had gone on in my life since we last had a heart to heart five years ago."

"So, you're going to try to get with the Gods?" she asked, whispering as softly as she could as we headed into the quad section and to the lunch area.

"Probably not," I said and shrugged. "I guess we will just have to wait and see what happens."

"I wish you luck," she muttered. "Lord knows I tried, myself, thinking maybe they might like a change of pace from these boring-ass white girls."

"Girls in general are so often boring," I agreed.

She scoffed. "Preaching to the choir here, girl."

We got into line for lunch, and I let out a breath to try to release the stress from my shoulders. Classes were easy, but that didn't mean they would remain that way.

Soon, I was sure I would be overwhelmed with work.

Or not, if the rumors I heard about school down here in the south were true. Some said they had horrible schooling, but who knew what I would experience.

"What kind of food do they have here? Grits?" I asked with a teasing smile.

She shrugged. "Sometimes."

My mouth dropped. "You're joking?"

She shook her head. "Nope. Sometimes we get grits."

"What about pizza?"

She laughed. "Pizza? We never have pizza." Her brow furrowed. "You got pizza at your school?"

I nodded. "Every single day we got pizza. Man, this is going to make me want to resume making my lunches at home beforehand."

"If you make your own lunch, make me one, too," she begged.

"Me, too," a deep voice said behind me.

We both turned, and I looked at the guy who had been sitting beside Branson in second period.

He held out his hand. "I'm Taylor."

I shook his hand. "Cameron."

"So, Cameron, who is your favorite so far?" he asked.

"Favorite?" I asked.

He smirked. "I see. You haven't met everyone yet. No worries. Tomorrow, you can tell me who your favorite is."

I looked at Tamara, but she was paying the cashier for her food and looking everywhere but at us.

"I don't know what you mean," I whispered.

He smiled. "You will."

With that ominous statement, I turned around to pay for the pasta and chicken nuggets I had deemed the most edible-looking food and followed Tamara to a long table which was mostly filled with a random assortment of kids.

I looked at the table where Branson and Taylor sat with another guy, whispering to each other.

"Those the Gods?" I asked Tamara.

She nodded.

As I watched them talking, I felt a deep sadness build within me. I'd been part of the popular crowd once and it hadn't worked out. I'd been part of the outcasts and that had been worse.

Would I find a place to just belong? A place I could just be myself?

I didn't know that I wanted to push myself to try to date the Gods, but where did that leave me?

It was only the first day of school, so I really needed to stop putting so much pressure on myself.

"Hey, Tamara," a guy said in a deep, but soft voice.

I looked at the guy who sat down across from us. He had bulging biceps, stylish hair, and a light goatee and mustache. Just at the edge of his shirt's collar, I saw what looked like a tattoo.

"Hey, Wade. This is Cameron. Cameron, this is Wade," Tamara introduced as she ate her food.

Wade held his hand out across the table, and I shook it.

"Nice to meet you," I said with a smile.

He returned my smile. "You, too."

"Are you a senior, too?" I asked while poking the chicken nuggets that now looked rather...oddly shaped.

"Yep. One last year and then I'm out!" he said, shouting a bit at the end, which earned us a few stares.

"You still saving up to move out of town with the guys?" Tamara asked.

Wade nodded, took a big bite out of the sandwich he'd pulled from his bag, and once he finished chewing said, "Yep. We've got a pretty good nest egg already."

"Where are you guys planning to move?" I asked around the bite of mushy macaroni and cheese.

"California," he said. "To one of the smaller towns there."

"It can be a sort of double-edged sword."

He scowled. "What do you mean?"

"Sure, it's nice to be in a small town, but there aren't many jobs there. They prioritize the local community for the jobs over new people. They can also be super prejudiced, even against other white people," I explained.

"Really?" Tamara asked. "Even over other white people?"

I nodded. "It's all about connections. Don't get me wrong, I still plan to move to one once I turn eighteen, but there are some drawbacks to it."

"How long did you live in California?" he asked me.

"My entire life up until a few weeks ago," I answered.

"You ever live in one of the small towns?" Tamara asked.

I nodded and cringed. "It was short-lived. They don't like outsiders, especially those who can't blend in. Not everyone was bad, and it could have been just that town, so I want to do research before I move to another one."

Wade exhaled. "We could blend in, but our biggest reason for leaving is so we don't have to pretend anymore."

"I'm sure you'd do fine," I whispered. "Don't let my opinions dissuade you. I'm just sharing my experience."

I hated when I opened my mouth and caused issues for people.

"Just ignore me," I added before shoveling food into my mouth.

"Hey, Cameron, why don't you come sit with us?" Branson asked, standing behind Wade who looked tense as hell.

I smiled politely. "Thank you, but I'm almost done anyways."

He winked, unperturbed by my denial. "You've always got a spot with us."

After he left, Tamara turned to me with wide eyes. "That was your chance, why didn't you go?"

I looked at my fork and whispered, "It's too early for me to decide on my place in this school. I don't know that I want to be part of the popular crowd again. That always comes with its own issues and drama. I'd rather stay low for a bit."

"Better be a bit nicer to Sylvia then," she whispered.

"Right," I whispered back and sighed.

Wade laughed. "Don't act so sad. All of us have to fake being nice to her all the time."

I scoffed. "I don't know that I'll be able to do that, but I would rather not be part of drama if I can help it."

"You're always welcome to eat with me," Wade said. "We can both sit as far from anyone else as possible."

I smiled at him. "Thanks. I appreciate it."

"We ran into Sean this morning," Tamara said.

"Again?" Wade asked.

Tamara laughed. "This time he ran into Cameron, too."

Wade sighed. "I apologize for my friend. He's a bit scatter-brained at times and doesn't watch where he is going. Did he hurt you?"

I shook my head, remembering the tattooed hottie. "Nope. You guys are friends?"

Wade nodded. "Best friends since I was in kindergarten. He's a year older, graduated last year."

"That's cool," I said, unsure what else to say.

"You have any long-term friends?" he asked with a wide smile.

I flinched and looked down at my plate, feeling my appetite disappear instantly. "No."

"Well, maybe you'll make some friends here," he said in a soft voice.

Yeah, not likely. I could have some fun acquaintances, but I wasn't going to have a best friend. Having a best friend just gave them lots of ammunition when they decided to stab you in the back later.

I liked my back unscathed.

CHAPTER THREE

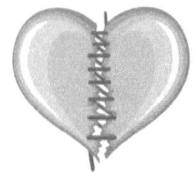

I managed to make it through the rest of the school day without embarrassing myself, which was quite an accomplishment.

Tamara had something to do after school, so I walked home by myself.

At four o'clock in the afternoon, the town was a bit busier, and I watched people going in and out of the stores with smiles on their faces.

"Hey," Wade said as he came up behind me.

I smiled at him. "Hey. Where are you off to?"

He tilted his head towards the store where I had run into Sean. "Coming to see Sean. You?"

"Oh, just headed home," I said. "You guys lived here your entire lives?"

He nodded. "Unfortunately."

"What's in that store anyway?" I asked as we stopped in front of it. There were crystal figurines in the windows, but I could also see books towards the back.

"It's an all-in-one store for visitors," he said. "Has

souvenirs, postcards, little figurines, and also books available that are secondhand."

"Any good books?" I asked.

He smirked. "Come inside and find out."

I chuckled. "Alright."

He pulled open the door, and I stepped inside. Sure enough, it was full of random gifts and things that tourists would purchase to take home to their loved ones as a gift. Far in the back were several shelves holding books of varying degrees of wear and a huge variety of topics.

I beelined towards the fiction section, all three shelves of it, and thumbed through them.

"Hey, Sean. How's it going?" Wade asked.

"Same as any other day," Sean answered. "Oh, hi. You're the girl I bumped into earlier with Tamara, right? Sorry about that."

I didn't turn around, my hand resting on a pristine edition of The Hobbit. "No worries." I pulled it out and felt my mouth drop at the minuscule price tag. How could they sell it for so cheap? I turned. "Is this the real price?"

Sean and Wade turned, stopping the whispering they had been doing behind my back.

Sean walked over, inspected the pencil marked cost inside the paperback. "Yes, only two dollars."

I set the book down, took off my backpack, and fished around inside for my spare change. I didn't ever have much money on me, but I usually had a couple of dollars in change. I pulled out the pennies and nickels I found, counting them out, then searched for more.

Sean set his hand on top of mine as I counted my change again. I looked up into his warm gaze. "Take it," he whispered.

"I don't have enough on me, but I can get more at home and—"

"You can have it. I'll pay for it," he said.

"No, it's okay. I can pay. I've read it before, but I don't own my own copy so I just wanted—"

He took the forty cents I'd pulled out, fished change out of his own pocket, and then put it inside the register. He held out the receipt, smiling wide. "Here."

I took it, sure I was blushing a deep tomato red. "Thanks."

"So, you enjoy your first day?" Wade asked me.

I shrugged. "It's not so bad for a small town." I looked up at the two of them. "I expected there to be a lot more guys in overalls, honestly."

They both laughed.

"You're always welcome in here," Sean said. "Not that many people come to this back section, so you can even come here and read."

I looked over at the four beanbag chairs arranged in a corner of the room. "You guys hang out here a lot?"

Wade shrugged. "When Sean's working, usually. It's a quiet place to do our homework and still get to be around each other."

It must have been nice to have friends like that. Friends that truly wanted to spend time with you.

I hugged the book to my chest and whispered, "Well, thank you for the book...and the offer. I have to get home before my mom sends the Coast Guard after me or something."

"See you tomorrow," Wade said.

I nodded and hurried out of the store.

Maybe this town wouldn't be so awful after all.

Maybe, just maybe, the guys here might be different.

"There she is," Branson said behind me. "Hey, Cameron."

I turned, waved with a smile, and called out, "Sorry, I got to get home to my mama. See you boys later."

All three of the Gods scowled at me, but before they could respond, I spun and ran as fast as my legs would take me.

I wasn't going to run from them forever, but I was going to try to give myself some time to actually get to know the guys here before moving forward on dating anyone. *If* I dated anyone at all.

Maybe Karen would forgive me if I immediately gave up chase of the guys she was clearly interested in?

Or, she might just make my life a little less hell-like. With girls like her, it was hard to tell.

I pushed open the door and called out, "Hi, Mom. I'm home."

Mom poked her head out of the kitchen and smiled. "How was your first day?"

I stroked my thumb over the book in my arms. "Good. How was your day?"

She shrugged. "Same old, same old. I'll have dinner ready in an hour. Do you want a snack?"

"Yes, please. They're feeding us gruel."

She laughed and shook her head. "You're overreacting."

"Mom, they've never had pizza for lunch, ever."

She shrugged. "You were spoiled."

"Can I make food to take for lunch instead of eating the school lunch?" I begged.

She smiled. "Sure. As long as you clean up your mess afterwards, I would love for you to spend more time in the kitchen."

Don't roll your eyes. Don't roll your eyes.

Mom was always trying to find ways to get me into the kitchen more so she could turn me into a proper housewife.

No, thank you. My goal was definitely not to become a housewife. Not that there was anything wrong with it, that just wasn't the life I wanted for myself.

"Any homework?" she asked as I sat on a bar stool at the kitchen counter.

I took the plate of apple slices from her and shook my head. "Nope. Today was all about the syllabus and what to expect in the coming months."

"You going to ace this year?" she asked.

I shrugged nonchalantly. "Possibly."

"Any cute boys?"

I laughed and shook my head. "Oh, yeah. A trio of them, but I am going to steer clear of that group."

"Oh, you met the Gods?" she asked.

My head whipped up as I looked at her, but she was wiping the counter with a rag and not looking at me.

"How did you know about them?"

She glanced at me, rolled her eyes, and resumed cleaning the counter. "I did my research when we came here. I wanted to be sure we weren't coming to the same type of school."

"There is something about them," I whispered.

She chuckled. "You say that about every hot guy you see."

I shook my head, chomped on an apple slice, and then said, "I'm going to try to avoid drawing attention to myself as much as possible. I'd like to stay clear of the popular girls getting mad that I drew their attention away. I don't want them to drain my blood or sacrifice me to make them prettier."

She scowled. "You've been reading paranormal books again, haven't you?"

I laughed nervously. "Maybe?"

"Girl, don't let those books go to your head, okay? There is nothing paranormal about this town."

I sighed. "Mom, I know. I wasn't meaning it literally. It was a joke."

She clenched the rag in her hands. "Be careful around those girls, okay? I hear they rule here and although I'm certain you could take them in a fight, that would only make things bad for you."

I popped another apple slice in my mouth and smiled. "You know I will."

She stared at me a moment longer and then nodded once and resumed cleaning.

I finished my apple in silence then hurried up the stairs to my room.

No sooner had I sat on my bed then something hit my window. I walked to the window and lifted it up with a grunt.

A pebble smacked me right between the eyes.

"Ow," I called out and rubbed the spot.

"Oh, shit. Sorry. Are you okay?" Wade called up to me.

I sat on the windowsill and stared down at him. "What are you doing here? Stalking me?"

He rubbed the back of his neck, and I admired the way his biceps flexed. "Um, I was wondering if you wanted to sit outside with me and Tamara while we read?"

"What?" I asked.

"We do it most nights. Just sit together and read books while enjoying the company of others," he said.

My mouth clenched into a tight line. Crap, was I encroaching on Tamara's territory? Did she have a thing for him and now I was getting in her way?

I really needed to talk to her.

"I'll come down, but I need to talk to Tamara first, okay?" I said.

He nodded, smiling wide, and disappeared around the side of the house.

"Mom, I'm going to go talk to the neighbor, Tamara," I called out. "We'll be outside so just yell when dinner is ready."

"Alright. Behave," she called back.

I hurried out of the house, across the lawn that was ten times as big as our last house's lawn, and to Tamara's backyard.

We didn't have fences, so it was sort of hard to know where our property ended and hers began, but it wasn't really important.

In the back of her house were a few different pieces of outdoor furniture: a love seat, a tire swing, and three wicker chairs.

Two of the chairs were taken up by Wade and Tamara, sitting right next to each other. Sean sat in another chair, fully engrossed in a book.

"Hey, um, Tamara? Can I talk to you a second?" I asked, scuffing the toe of my shoe against a rock on the ground.

She put the bookmark in her book, closed it, and walked over to me. "What's up?" she asked.

I pulled her farther away from the area, out of earshot, and asked, "Do you have a thing for Wade?"

Her eyes widened, and she looked back at him and then at me. "What? Hell no. Why would you even ask that?"

"Well, he said you guys hang out a lot, and I didn't want to step on your toes or anything and..." I trailed off as she started laughing.

What started as a light laugh turned into deep, belly laughs and then she fell to the ground on her side, gasping for breath as she laughed.

I covered my face with my hands.

"Girl, you are hilarious," she gasped, stood, and wiped the tears from her eyes. She set her hand on my shoulder and said, "I appreciate you asking, but no. I don't like any of the boys at our school, or Sean. They are all free game."

"Really?" I asked.

She nodded. "I've got a man, but don't let my parents hear that. He's over in the town to the east."

"Swear?" I asked.

She draped her arm around my shoulders, steered me back to the little sitting area, and pushed me down into the love seat beside the chair Wade sat in. "Swear. You can even try for those Gods if you want."

I pulled out my current book, settled into the love seat, and buried myself in the story.

"Hey," I heard Wade say.

"Hey," Tamara greeted.

"Evening," a new voice greeted Tamara, but I was too engrossed in the epic battle going on to pull myself out of it to look at them.

"Don't mind her, she's entranced by the battle going on," Tamara said. "I've read that book and trust me, it's just getting good, so she won't be out of there for at least twenty minutes."

"Who's this?" the new person asked.

"New neighbor," Tamara answered. "She..."

Her voice faded away as the main character threw herself on the blade of the enemy to save her mate, losing her wings to save his life. Tears sprang to my eyes, and I put my hand up over my mouth to keep from sobbing out loud as she realized that she would never fly again despite being a demigod. She didn't have the ability to regenerate wings after a divine blade was used.

"She's crying," Wade whispered.

"She's going to fit in so well," Sean said and chuckled.

"She did it for her mate," Tamara whispered. "She sacrificed her wings for him and she would do it a million times over."

I looked up, tears streaming down my face. "I know! If only they had listened to her and been more cautious."

Tamara shook her head. "It wouldn't have mattered. Either one of her mates would have tried to protect her, which would have forced her to protect them, or something else would have happened. She had to sacrifice a part of herself to prove she wanted to keep them. To prove she loved them."

"She proved that already!" I argued and wiped at my face. "Dammit, sorry. This isn't how I generally like to make my first impressions."

The new guy held out his hand from the chair beside me. "I'm Noah."

"Cameron," I said and smiled. "You can call me Cam, though."

Tamara narrowed her eyes. "Why does he get to call you Cam, but I don't?"

I laughed. "I meant all of you can call me Cam. Calm down, girl."

"So, Cam, how are you liking our town?" Noah asked. He had a beard and a few scattered tattoos on his forearms.

"It's actually a lot nicer than I thought it was going to be," I admitted. I glanced at Wade and whispered, "And the bookstore is better than I thought it would be."

"You thought it was going to be all religious books or nonfiction, didn't you?" Wade asked.

I blushed as I nodded. "Yeah."

Everyone laughed.

"It used to be," Wade said. "Until I started buying books from garage sales and putting them in there."

"That's one of our weekend activities," Wade said. "We go around to the garage sales and try to find books to buy that would do well in the store.

"Or in our own bookshelves," Noah said with a smirk.

That sounded like a lot of fun, and I really hoped that someday I might be able to go with them.

"So, you guys do this every night?" I asked, moving over on

the love seat so there was room for another person to sit beside me.

Everyone nodded.

"Do you mind if I come join you some nights?" I asked. "I feel like I'm totally crashing tonight."

Tamara laughed. "You are welcome here any night you want. My parents are ecstatic that you're here, even if your hair is purple."

I touched my hair. For a bit I had forgotten that it was purple. "It'll fade soon."

"I like it," Noah said with a wink. "It suits you."

"It's nice to have a bit of color in this town for once," Wade said.

Tamara smacked his arm.

He cringed, rubbing it. "You know what I meant!" he yelled.

We all laughed and for the first time in years, I felt like I might actually be somewhere I belonged. How could I feel that way on my first day?

Normally, it took me months to find people I got along with.

"So, what else do you guys do for fun in this tiny town?" I asked.

"We have fun here?" Noah asked.

Tamara rolled her eyes. "Don't let these boys fool you. They go party it up with the other idiots all the time."

"Not all the time," Sean muttered.

"You meet the Gods?" Noah asked me.

I nodded while looking at my hands in my lap. "Yeah. I met them."

"Oh, someone else who is put off by them? Now that is interesting," he said.

"Are they...violent?" I asked softly. Some schools had

brutes who got away with everything because they were attractive.

"Violent? No, not usually," Tamara answered, but the silence from the guys made me wonder if there was something she didn't know about.

"I take it you didn't have good experiences with some of the people in your last town?" Noah asked me.

Sean's hands clenched into fists in his lap, and Wade stared at me as he waited for me to answer.

I stood. "Uh, it was nice meeting you all, but I need to get home." I hurried towards my house just before Mom started yelling my name for dinner.

"You scared her off!" Wade snapped behind me.

"Can't you learn to read people better?" Tamara asked and sighed.

"There you are," Mom said with a smile as I walked up the steps, my hands fisted in the bottom of my shirt.

I nodded and rushed past her. "I'm going to put my book away and clean up, then I'll be down for dinner, okay?"

"Okay," she said, her voice soft.

I shut and locked the bathroom door behind me, turned on the sink water, then slumped down to the floor, face in my hands, and sobbed into them.

Why? Why was I still running away from people when they just asked me a simple question?

They hadn't threatened me or anything. They'd just made an observation and asked me a question.

I didn't have to say anything. I could have just nodded and then steered the conversation away if I wanted to.

Why did I have to run? Why did I have to make myself look like a bigger freak than I really was?

I just wanted to make some friends. Friends I could spend time with doing normal high school kid things.

Instead, I ran away from them as soon as they asked me a few questions.

Dammit. Dammit. Dammit.

Dinner was a somber affair, and I went to bed as soon as I finished eating.

Mom didn't push me to help her clean or ask me any questions, likely able to tell that I was upset.

Something flew through the window and landed on my stomach.

I sat up, looking at the small pebble in my hand. "Again?" I asked softly.

"Hey!" Wade called.

I sat in the windowsill, but kept my head turned inside. "What's up?"

"Can I walk with you and Tamara tomorrow?" he asked.

I turned and looked at him. "What?"

He pointed to the house about a mile down the road. "I live there. Can I walk to school with you two tomorrow? Tamara told me I had to ask you."

Why did he have to ask me?

"It's a free world and this is your town," I answered with a shrug.

He stared at me expectantly.

"Yes, you can walk with us," I said.

His smile was like being blasted with a gust of warm air on the beach. I gasped softly, certain I was blushing again.

"Awesome. I'll see you tomorrow. Night, Purple Girl."

"Night," I called softly, but he was already running across the field, hopping a fence to get to the road.

This town continued to surprise me.

With a smile, I lay back down and fell asleep.

I'd forgotten to set my alarm for earlier to give myself time to make a lunch, but Mom surprised me with a lunch pre-made for me on the counter with a heart on the brown paper sack.

I smiled as I put it in my backpack and hurried outside, rushing to Tamara's front door where she was putting on her shoes.

I waved at her mother. "Morning, Ma'am."

Her mother was a plump, African American woman, with the most perfect skin and hair I had ever seen on a human being.

"You sure she isn't a goddess?" I asked Tamara as she came outside.

"You know I am," her mother yelled after us.

I waved to her, and Tamara rolled her eyes at me. "You're just trying to earn some brownie points with my mom since you dyed your hair all crazy."

I hiked my backpack up higher. "So?"

"Hey!" Wade called as he ran up to us. He stopped, put his hands on his knees, and panted. "Sorry, I'm late."

"It's okay. We were just going to leave without you," Tamara said and started walking.

I looked from Wade to Tamara and jogged to catch up to her, then slowed down to walk with her.

Wade walked on my left, on the road side.

"So, day one is down. It's all downhill from here, right?" he asked me.

I scoffed. "I wish."

"Did you read more of your book last night?" Tamara asked.

I shook my head. "No."

She groaned. "Come on, you have got to finish it so we can talk about it!"

I laughed. "Alright. I'll finish it tonight at your house after school."

She nodded. "Okay."

"Hey, um, just so you know, Noah didn't mean anything by his question," Wade said.

I shoved my feelings down and nodded. "It's alright."

"No, it's not. Stop talking about it, you dunderhead," Tamara snapped and smacked Wade on the back of his head. "You three are so damn dense sometimes, I swear. It's no wonder why none of you could keep a girlfriend."

"I'm sorry," Wade said as he rubbed the back of his head.

"Not me. Her!" Tamara snapped.

He turned and said, "I'm sorry." Then, right there in the middle of town, bowed to me. "I'm sincerely sorry."

"Stand up," I hissed. "It's fine. Seriously. Stop bowing!"

"You have to say you forgive me," he said, holding his position.

More adults were stopping from their shopping and morning activities to stare at us.

"I forgive you," I screeched, grabbed his arm, and dragged him forward. "Come on!"

It wasn't until we were in front of the school that I realized I was still holding his arm.

I dropped it and cleared my throat. "Sorry."

"So, are you ready for PE?" Tamara asked.

"Let me guess, baseball?" I murmured.

She laughed. "It's almost like you understand how these small-town people think. Yes, baseball. All of the baseball and then later in the year, flag football."

I froze. "What? Th-they m-make us p-play..." I couldn't even finish the question.

"It's okay, I'm in your class," Wade said. "I won't let anything happen to you."

I heard him, but the words wouldn't process.

The last time I had done flag football, I'd gone to the hospital. Would Mom write me a note? Excuse me from...

Warm arms wrapped around me and a sense of safety and security settled over me.

I closed my eyes and let my head rest on the soft pillows there. Warmth and security. Something I hadn't experienced in at least a decade.

"What the hell is this? It's been one day?" Sylvia asked.

I jerked back a step, my gaze going up to Wade's face as realization hit me.

He had been hugging me.

I'd been wrapped up in his arms with my head on his chest.

"I'm s-s-sorry," I stammered and backed away from him.

Tamara wrapped her arms around my shoulders and held me in place. "Beat it, Sylvia. We know you don't understand how friendship works so it's okay that you also don't know what affection looks like."

My heart hammered in my chest, and I tried to calm it, but it wouldn't listen to me.

Tamara steered me into the nearest bathroom, shoved me into a small stall, ignoring the looks of the other girls, and gripped me by the shoulders. "Focus on me."

I nodded and licked my lips. "I am."

"You good?"

"Almost," I gasped, took a few breaths, then regretted it since I was in the bathroom and started gagging.

She laughed, and we walked out of the bathroom laughing.

"You okay?" Wade nodded.

I smiled and nodded. "Yep. Let's go to class."

Without any other comments, we made our way into the school and to first period. Much like the previous day, we had a fairly easy time with very little learning and more of an expla-nation of what to expect.

At lunch, I pulled out my sack lunch and Tamara snickered. "Mama made your lunch?"

I shrugged. "I forgot to set my alarm to make it myself. There is no way I am going to eat the crap they tell you is food here."

Wade chuckled while he scarfed down the "food" himself.

Maybe I should make him a lunch, too, so he didn't have to eat this gruel.

"Hey, Cameron," Taylor said as he came to stand behind Wade.

"Hello, Taylor," I greeted and then shoved my sandwich in my mouth to take a bite. "'Sup?" I asked around the bite of food.

"Come sit with us," he said, not an offer, but an order.

I swallowed. "But I'm already here."

"Please?" he asked and batted his eyelashes.

"Go ahead," Tamara whispered to me while she bent to pretend to pick something up.

"Okay," I said, smiled at Taylor, and gathered my food and backpack to follow him.

Every eye in the cafeteria was on us as we walked back to the table with the other two Gods.

I sat down and smiled at the other two. "What's up, guys?" I asked.

"We heard you've been spending time with Wade and his trio of hipsters."

Hipsters? These fools had no idea what a hipster was.

"I mean, you could call them nerds, but not hipsters," I said. "For one, none of them folds their pant legs up or wears skinny jeans. Also, none have curled mustaches or even a tiny bit of wax in their facial hair."

My rambling made them scowl and their mouths close.

Good, you all need to know you aren't the smartest boys in the school even if you are hot.

"Since they like reading, you could call them nerds, but that would make me a nerd, too, so I guess I'm just finding the group I'm meant to be part of," I continued and then chewed on the last bit of my sandwich.

"You don't belong with them," Branson said. "You belong with us."

I swallowed and looked at them all before asking, "You? But, you're the popular guys."

"And you are the California girl with colorful hair," Taylor said.

"You guys play on the football team, right?" I asked.

They nodded.

I wiped my hands on my pants. "Then you are way out of my league. You should be going after people like Karen and her cronies."

"Karen?" Taylor asked.

I cringed. I had forgotten her actual name.

"Look, I really appreciate your offer, but I am not going to be a good fit for you three," I whispered.

"And you think the nerds are a better fit?" Branson asked. "That they have more to offer you than us?"

I shook my head. "No, I think that I'm not a good fit for anyone. I plan to be out of here as soon as I turn eighteen. I am a mess and I don't expect anyone to be able to truly understand me or the craziness that goes on in my head. I'm a freak and you, Gods, deserve goddesses. You'll find them, trust me, there are plenty of girls wishing to find guys like you out there. You would be snatched up within minutes at my old school."

"But not by you," the third guy, whose name I hadn't learned, said.

"I won't sully you in that way," I whispered. "So, no."

"You think very low of yourself," he whispered.

"No, I'm just honest. Thank you for letting me sit with you, but I'm going to leave before I tarnish your reputation any more than I already have," I said, stood, and walked out of the cafeteria.

I had hoped the rest of the day would go easy, but then third period came. Physical Education.

They didn't have clothes for us yet, but they didn't care. They made us do the workout in our regular clothes and then had us run half a mile.

I jogged around the track, muttering about stupid backwoods schools the entire time.

"You doing alright?" Tamara asked as she ran by me.

I stuck my tongue out at her, but didn't reply. I had stamina to run, but I wasn't quick.

When I had finally made it, I panted off to the side and chugged some water from the fountain.

"You prefer long distances?" the teacher, a fit Caucasian man in workout clothes, asked.

I nodded. "Yeah. I'm not much for sprinting."

"Ever consider joining the track team?" he asked.

I shrugged.

"If you want to, just let me know," he said and then turned to yell at one of the slower students.

I could join the team, but that would mean mandatory after school practices and races where I could let someone down if I lost.

I didn't know if I wanted to deal with that in such a small town. Letting down a town of one million was one thing, letting down a town of five hundred was completely different.

"Nice work today," Noah said from beside me.

I turned and looked at him. "Oh, hey, Noah. I didn't realize you were part of our school, too."

He smirked. "I prefer to stay hidden as much as necessary."

"I understand that," I muttered, turned and sat on the grass as we waited for the rest of the class to finish their run.

He sat beside me, leaning back on his arms and I spied tattoos.

"Do you all have tattoos?" I asked.

He glanced at his arm and then nodded. "Yeah."

"Lucky," I grumbled.

He smiled. "Want a tattoo?" he asked.

I nodded. "I've wanted one for years."

"What kind of tattoo would you get?" he asked.

I smirked. "Guess."

He shook his head while chuckling. "No way. Last time I did that, the girl slapped me in the face before walking away and calling me all sorts of curse words."

I arched a brow at him. "You said tramp stamp, didn't you?"

He laughed while nodding.

I shook my head. "Boys."

"Seriously, though. What would you get?"

I looked up at the sky, squinting at the sun. "That's a conversation I don't like to have so early in a friendship."

"Oh, is this a friendship?" he asked.

I shrugged, still not looking at him. "You tell me. I'd like for it to be one, but that's really up to you and your friends, I think. I'm here at least for the year. If you want to be friends, it seems like we might be able to be friends, or at least acquaintances."

"I'd like to be your friend, I think. You seem better than the Tiffanys over there," he said.

I looked in the direction he was and saw Sylvia and her friend. I laughed at his term for them.

"Yeah, they're something alright."

He held out his hand. "I'm Noah. It's nice to become friends with you, Cameron."

I shook his hand. "Cam."

"Cam," he repeated while we shook hands.

Our smiles didn't last as long as I had hoped due to Sylvia coming over.

"Hey, new girl," she snapped.

I sighed and looked up at her. "How can I help you?"

She put her hands on her tiny waist and said, "You can help me by keeping away from the Gods."

I shrugged. "They invited me to their table. Trust me, it wasn't me who instigated that interaction. And don't fret, Sylvia, I told them they should be more interested in you than me."

The girl to her right, a petite blond with a flat chest, let her mouth drop open at that.

"I don't need your help," Sylvia said and flipped her hair over her shoulder.

"Of course you don't, Princess," I said and smiled. "You'll snag those boys sure as whipped cream on pumpkin pie!" I put as much enthusiasm into the words as I could.

She scoffed. "You are so weird. I don't know why they're even bothering to give you any attention."

I shrugged. "Me neither. Could be that they haven't had a taste of my forbidden forest?"

My suggestion made her and her cronies blush.

Noah threw his head back as he laughed.

"Shut up, Noah," she snapped. "No one wants trash to talk."

I stood up and asked, "Then why are you still talking?"

I could handle a lot, but I could not handle people treating others poorly. I know, totally backwards, but I called it the Mom Syndrome. If someone else was in trouble, I became the de facto leader and had to stick up for them.

She sneered. "So, she does have fangs. Good. You'll need them."

"No, I won't. I don't have any interest in your games. Just leave us alone," I urged her.

She stepped closer, but right when she opened her mouth, Noah grabbed my wrist and pulled me away from her.

"Time to head in," he said.

I looked down at his hand on my wrist and exhaled, feeling my pounding heart trying to free itself from the cage of my ribs. "Shit."

We walked around the cafeteria-slash-gym and he released me, then dropped down so we were eye to eye. "You alright?"

I nodded, shook my head, and then nodded again.

He chuckled. "I was pretty surprised when you jumped in there and defended me. I appreciate it, but that's not something you need to do. I can handle her and her little crew of followers."

"Sorry, it's not something I really control," I whispered and rubbed at my chest.

"I'm glad you stood up to her, though. She deserves to know she isn't the queen of this school," he whispered.

"Hey, Noah?" I asked.

"Yeah?" he asked, stepping closer.

"Catch me?" I asked and then the world went dark.

CHAPTER FOUR

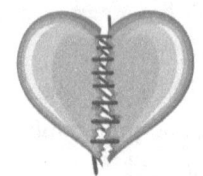

"What did you do to her?" I heard Tamara ask.

"It wasn't me. It was Sylvia. She was being her usual self and insulted me and then Cam stuck up for me. But then it overwhelmed her and she passed out," Noah said.

Someone was petting my hair, and I really liked it.

"Mmm," I mumbled and snuggled closer to the warmth at my back.

"She's waking up," my pillow said in the voice of Wade.

I jerked upright with a screech and clutched my head. "Sorry. Sorry. Sorry."

"Easy," he whispered. "It's okay."

"Sorry," I whispered again.

Noah knelt on his knees before me and took my hands away from my head. "Hey. It's okay."

I exhaled and nodded. "Class over?" I asked, my hands shaking in his.

He nodded. "Basically. I think there's still like two minutes until the bell rings. You okay to stand? Do you want me to grab your bag?"

"I'll get it," I snapped and tried to stand, but stumbled.

"I got it," Tamara said and jogged away.

I sat back down and buried my face in my knees. Crap.

"So, do you have a favorite snack?" Wade asked.

"Huh?" I asked without moving or opening my eyes.

"It's my turn to bring snacks to our reading session. Do you have a favorite snack?"

"Cheesy Balls," I whispered.

"Perfect!" he said. "I've got a tub of those I can bring."

"What do you like to drink?" Noah asked.

"Whiskey," I mumbled.

"Huh?" he asked.

"Lemonade," I said.

"My mama makes the best lemonade in three counties," Tamara said as she returned. "I'll ask her to make some. I'm sure she'll be glad to make some for her worshipper."

"I'm not a worshipper," I argued, letting my hands drop. "I just accept that she is a goddess."

"She is a goddess," Wade said.

Tamara smacked him. "Don't be talking about my mama like that!"

"But she just did," he argued.

"She's not talking about how plump my mama is," Tamara snapped and put her hands on her hips, my backpack and hers on her shoulders.

"Well, a little bit," I said and shrugged. "True goddesses have to have a bit of mass to them."

Tamara laughed and held out my bag. "That's the truth right there. Why do they always show goddesses as twigs? Have you seen statues of the Greek goddesses over there? They have rolls. True goddesses aren't thin as a rail. They have figures."

I looked down at my thin body and said, "Yeah, I knew I wasn't a goddess the first time I saw an Aphrodite statue."

Tamara draped her arm around my shoulders. "Not everyone can be an immortal being. Some of us have to be the worshippers."

"I guess at least I'm still useful," I said. "I could be a temple maiden."

"We should have a toga party," Wade whispered to Noah.

Tamara and I shook our heads. "No."

Noah laughed, stood, brushed off his pants, and then helped me stand up. "Come on, let's go."

I brushed myself off after I was up and smiled up at him. "Thank you."

He nodded once, released me, and then turned to talk to the other two.

Was this what friendship was like? True friendship?

Once school was over, we headed to Sean's shop, where we waited until he was finished with his shift before we all went to the little convenience store to grab snacks, and then go to Tamara's to read and hang out.

We walked out of the store, laughing at something Wade had said, only to be stopped by the Gods.

I swallowed as I took them in. In the evening, they seemed even more gorgeous.

"Cameron," Branson called, smiling wide. "I was hoping to run into you."

I felt the guys move closer to me and wasn't sure if I should let them, or tell them to back off so they didn't get involved.

"What's up?" I asked and took a step closer to him.

"Are you busy Friday night?" he asked.

"Actually, she is," Noah said, stepped forward, and draped his arm around my shoulders, pulling me against his side.

Branson scowled.

Taylor walked up, smiling. "Well, why don't you just come

with her, Noah? You know every year we hold the beginning of the year bonfire? Just bring her as your date."

"You know we don't usually attend that," Wade said.

Branson shrugged. "It's your last year, so why not live a little? All of you come. Even you, Sean. We don't care that you graduated last year. Come hang out."

"Um, we'll consider it," I said and nudged Noah's side. "Have a good night, guys."

Noah pivoted, taking me with him, but none of us talked again until we were in Tamara's backyard.

"What was that about?" Sean snapped. "Since when do they want us there?"

"Why does it feel like a trap?" Noah asked, finally letting me go.

I sat heavily into the love seat and immediately chugged the water glass Tamara handed me.

"Mom's making lemonade," she whispered. "So, just give her a few minutes."

"What happens at this bonfire?" I asked.

"The normal high school stuff. Drinking, fighting, flirting, kissing, and all that," Tamara said.

"You've been?" Wade asked her.

"No, I have," Sean said. "I told her about it."

"When did you go?" Wade asked.

"My first year here," Sean answered. "I didn't really have much fun, so I never went again."

"I've been to parties before, ones that turned into absolute craziness, but I'm not a fan of them usually."

"It is your choice," Sean said. "You don't have to go."

"It's not like they're dangerous," Tamara said. "They're just trying to get the new pretty girl to come. Standard operating procedure."

"If you do go, I'll go with you," Noah said.

"Me, too," Wade said with a nod.

"Let's just read," Tamara said. "We don't need to think about all this right now. It's only Tuesday. We can forget about all that, and Cam can make her decision Friday night."

I sat back down, but despite wanting to finish the story I was reading, I couldn't force myself to pull the book from my bag and start reading it.

I could only think about the Gods and this event. Were they planning something or was I just being overly cautious because of my past experiences? Maybe they really were just being nice and there was nothing nefarious going on.

Two days. Dammit. Two damn days. That's all I had lasted before some potential drama started.

I tried so hard to stay out of it.

Normally, when drama always surrounded a person it was because they started it. Was it my fault? Did I somehow cause this? Was there some way to stop it? To help my friends get away from it?

No, I had to be overreacting. This was a small town and if those guys were psychos, Tamara would have known and warned me.

They were likely just being nice and inviting me to the party and since my friends had been with me, extended the invite to them as well.

I didn't want to go, so I would just skip it.

"Here," Wade said and held out a bowl of Cheesy Balls.

I took them and smiled up at him. "Thanks."

Sean sat on the love seat beside me with a drink in one hand and a book in the other.

I scooted over to ensure he had plenty of room and then started talking about the book I was reading with Tamara.

To my dismay, she refused to give me any spoilers and after

a few arguments, I pulled out my book to finish it so I could argue fully about the series once I had finished it.

"Cameron!" Mom yelled. "Dinner."

I put my bookmark in, said goodnight to everyone, and hurried home.

"You've been awfully quiet today," Tamara commented at lunch the next day.

I shrugged. "Not much to say, I guess."

"Are you sure you're not holding out on me?" she asked and nudged me with her elbow.

"I'm fine," I said and gave her my best smile possible.

"Right," she said, drawing out the word.

"You coming over tonight?" Wade asked.

I nodded. "Yep. I'll be there."

"Me, too," Noah said before sitting beside me.

"You're late. Everything alright?" Wade asked Noah.

Noah nodded. "Just helping the teacher with a little bit of a side project for extra credit."

I felt eyes on me and turned. Sure enough, the Gods were looking at me.

Branson winked at me.

I gave him a small smile and then resumed eating my lunch.

There had to be a way I could talk to them in a safe place, but still without anyone else around to hear what I was going to say to them to try to gauge their intentions properly.

"So, you want Cheesy Balls again tonight?" Noah asked.

I shook my head. "Just whatever you normally bring is fine. I'm not picky."

"Okay," he said and started shoveling his food into his mouth.

Somehow, he ate his entire lunch before the bell rang.

"I'm going to use the restroom and then go to class," I told the trio. "I'll meet you there."

"Okay," Tamara said.

We split up, and I hurried to the restroom and then out to find the Gods.

Thankfully, they were nearby, leaning against a wall, talking together.

"Hey," I said as I came up to them.

They smiled down at me.

"Hey," Taylor said.

"So, this party on Friday, what's it like?" I asked.

"Oh, you know, just a bunch of kids getting together and having fun," Branson said with a shrug.

"You considering going?" Taylor asked, his smile hopeful.

I shrugged. "Maybe. I might just come alone, though."

They exchanged a look and all smiled wide.

"Sounds good to us," Branson said.

"Well, I guess you'll know for sure Friday night whether I come or not," I said and shrugged like it was no big deal. "I've been to my fair share of parties, and I won't know until that day if I feel like going or not."

"You should really come," Branson said. "We'd love a chance to get to know you better."

I smiled. "I'll consider it. Later."

With a wave, I hurried through the campus towards my next class, freezing a moment when I saw Noah standing outside of his classroom, watching me go by.

Had he seen me with the Gods? Would he be upset that I was talking to them? I had to make sure he knew I wasn't doing anything bad or talking about them behind their backs to the Gods.

People made a lot of assumptions, myself included at times, and I wanted to make sure my new friends didn't view me as shifty or untrustworthy from the start.

Tamara looked at me as I came into the classroom and sat beside her. "You alright?"

I nodded and smiled. "Yep."

Branson sat beside me, slinging his backpack on top of his desk as he did.

She glanced at him and then at me and then arched her brow.

I sighed and dropped my head forward. "I'll tell you tonight, alright?"

She scoffed. "Damn straight you will."

Branson slid a piece of paper across his desk to mine.

I looked at him, but his eyes were focused on the teacher, so I took the paper and opened it. It had three phone numbers with three names. The Gods' phone numbers.

Whoa.

I re-folded it and slid it into my front pocket of my jeans. I did not want anyone else to get their hands on this. Especially not one of the guys tonight.

A girl had to keep her options open and dammit, if these hotties wanted to allow me to keep them as an option, then so be it!

I didn't need to be popular. I could just be an acquaintance they chatted with on occasion.

That was okay, right?

Right.

Totally.

Most likely what would happen is they would lose interest in me relatively soon when they realized I wouldn't put out. I may have been from California and I may not have been a virgin, but that didn't mean I was going to be a slut.

If they were like most guys, they'd lose interest quickly.

After school ended, we met up with the guys, headed to get Sean, and then to Tamara's house.

It was nice to have a ritual like this already. One that involved me being able to relax and just chill.

"Help me get the drinks," Tamara ordered me and dragged me into the house. Once in the kitchen she asked, "So, what did the Gods want with you?"

"Apparently, they want to get to know me better despite me telling them that I wasn't good enough for their godliness."

Her eyes widened. "You did not say that to them?"

I nodded. "I did. But they want to be friends, so..." I shrugged. "What does it hurt, right?"

She chuckled. "I'd be fine with being friends if I were you, too. I mean, as long as you don't let them tempt you or anything, you might actually benefit from their protection, you know?"

I hadn't even thought of that. That was a really good point.

"Right," I said, like I had already thought of that.

We grabbed the glasses and pitcher of lemonade and returned to the others.

Sean sat beside me on the love seat again. "Hey," he greeted when I sat down beside him.

"Hey," I said.

"How was school?" he asked.

I shrugged. "Another day in paradise."

"The Gods pestering you?" Noah asked from his seat beside me. He wasn't even looking at me, his nose buried in his book.

"No," I answered, but said nothing else.

He put his bookmark in and turned to face me. "We need to talk."

I tensed. "Uh, about?"

He tilted his head towards the tire swing. "Please?"

Everyone else was looking back and forth between each other with scowls.

I stood and followed Noah away from the group so we could talk privately.

"What's up?" I asked, gripping my left elbow with my right hand and being sure to leave at least six feet of space between us.

"If they're pestering you, you can tell us," he said. "We can talk to them and let them know that they're upsetting you. They're not the smartest, but they aren't usually malicious towards girls."

"No, they're not pestering me," I said.

"Then what? You're actually considering dating them?" he asked with a scowl.

"No, but they want to be friends and asked to talk more to get to know me better," I said softly.

"You need to be careful with them," he said taking a step closer to me.

I took a step back, my heart thundering. "Stop."

He stopped moving and held his hands up. "I'm not going to hurt you, Cam."

"They said they just want to be friends. Look, I know, there are plenty of awful people in the world. Trust me, I really freaking know. I'm going to keep my distance and protect myself. Don't worry. I won't let them hurt me."

He lowered his hands. "I wish you would talk to me. I know we just met, but..." he let his words trail off and I didn't know what to say to that.

"I promise I'm not going to talk to them about you guys. Okay? Can we go back?" I asked it in the softest voice I could.

"Yeah," he said and nodded once.

I hurried back, taking my spot next to Sean, but this time I scooted closer to him so I would be a bit farther away from Noah.

"Everything good?" Sean asked.

"Yep. Everything's good," Noah said in a cheerful voice.

I pulled out my book and resumed reading, ignoring the uncomfortable silence around us.

This is what I had been worried about. I had been worried I would screw up their dynamic that had been fine for years before I came.

"Chips?" Sean asked and held out the open bag in his hand.

I took one and smiled before biting it in half. "Thanks."

He nodded and turned back to his book, too.

I looked over at him, studying him while he was engrossed in his reading.

He really was handsome. And muscular.

Did he workout? Or was it just from his day to day life? Could you get muscles like that from moving boxes around the store?

"Drool," Tamara said around a fake cough.

I leveled her with a glare, but focused back on my book. I shouldn't have been staring at him like that with the others right next to us.

"Cameron!" Mom yelled.

I sighed, put my bookmark in, and put the book in my backpack. "Sorry, time to head in."

"See you tomorrow," Tamara said with a wave, a chip in her hand.

"Night, Cam," Sean said with a smile.

"Night," Noah and Wade called.

I nodded and hurried home.

As awkward as it had been earlier, it was still nice with them.

Just don't expect anything other than basic friendship. That's what I had to keep telling myself.

All I wanted was the base level friendship package. That's it.

Right.

Maybe if I told myself that a hundred times it would stick.

I knew myself and knew it wouldn't be long before I started falling into my old ways and allowing feelings to develop.

I was a sucker and always would be.

CHAPTER FIVE

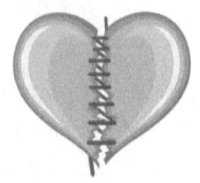

"What do you mean you didn't text them?" Tamara gaped as I finished putting my shoes on.

I shrugged. "I didn't want to seem needy or too anxious to talk to them."

She groaned. "You are hopeless."

"So, you would have messaged them right away?" I asked.

"Duh," she said and rolled her eyes.

"I've been in that situation before and it didn't work out well for anyone. I'm just trying to play it cool. If I feel like texting them, I will. If not..." I shrugged.

"Lord help me," she muttered.

We headed outside and Wade was already waiting for us. "Hey," he said with a smile.

"Hey," we greeted back.

"How's it going?" he asked.

"It's yet another glorious day in the Land of Promise," I said in my best pastor voice.

Tamara and Wade laughed loudly.

We started to walk by Sean's store, and I looked inside for

him to wave, but didn't see him. I turned to ask where he was right as he slammed into my side.

"Oof," I grunted and started to fall.

Sean caught me, wrapping me up in his arms, both of us half bent over like he was dipping me in a dance. "Good morning, Cam."

I smiled. "Morning, Sean. Nice to bump into you so early."

He helped me stand upright and sighed. "At least you didn't fall this time."

I chuckled. "Right. Any improvement is good."

"We have to hurry," Tamara said. "Cam made us run late as it is, and we don't have time to dally around."

I stuck my tongue out at her. "She's right, though."

"See you tonight?" he asked me.

I shrugged. "What else would I do?"

He waved, and we walked a bit faster towards the school.

"Was Noah rude to you last night?" Wade asked.

I shook my head. "No, he was just worried about me. He was trying to be a good friend, but just startled me a bit is all. No harm done. We all have to learn how to interact with each other."

"Right," he said softly and gripped his backpack's straps.

"Hey," Noah called out.

We stopped and turned to wait for him.

He jogged to catch up and started talking to Wade about something having to do with orcs that I didn't understand, so I tuned them out.

"They're talking about their gaming session," Tamara whispered.

"What game?" I asked her.

Both of their heads whipped up.

She sighed. "Now you've done it."

"You've never heard of Beasts and Bossfights?" Noah asked.

I shook my head. "What console is it on?"

"It's a paper and pen game," Wade said.

"Oh!" I gasped. "I've heard of this one. You create a character and use dice to determine what happens, right?"

They both nodded.

"Would...would you want to try it?" Wade asked softly.

I nodded my head vigorously. "I really would."

Noah smiled. "I think I have a character sheet in my bag. I can talk to you about it during lunch."

"Or after school," Tamara suggested. "So I can ignore you all with my book."

He chuckled. "She played with us once and died almost immediately. She's refused to play ever since."

"Three days!" she screeched. "I spent three days working on my character, her backstory, and finding a picture that looked like her and you killed her in one day. One encounter. One monster. Dead. Failed saving rolls. Permanently dead."

I tried to smother my smile, but it came anyway. "I'm sorry, that sounds awful."

"You still want to play it, don't you?" she asked with a scoff. "You are a glutton for punishment. Don't say I didn't warn you."

"Maybe I'll make three characters, that way I'll have a backup, just in case mine gets killed right away, too."

"That's what I have," Wade said.

"I can let you borrow my book to read over the rules," Noah said.

"Sure," I said and smiled at him.

The school day went by pretty fast and it went smoothly until the very end.

"Hey," Taylor called from behind me.

"I'll meet you at the house," I told Tamara.

She winked at me. "Go get 'em, girl."

I rolled my eyes. "Just friends, remember?"

Noah and Wade scowled, but Tamara looped her arms through theirs and pulled them away.

I turned back around and smiled up at the three Gods. "Hello, boys. What's up?"

"We thought maybe he messed up and didn't give you our correct numbers," Kieran, the third of the Gods, a blond haired, blue eyed southern gentleman if there ever was one, said.

I chuckled. "Well, possibly, but I didn't try to message or call any of you, so I'm not sure."

"Oh," Branson said, looking a bit shocked. They likely expected me to jump at the chance to call them.

"Sorry," I said with a shrug. "Was a bit busy last night."

"With them?" Taylor asked, looking over my head.

"With Tamara and our friends," I said with a nod.

"What do you guys do?" Kieran asked, his head slightly tilted to the side.

"Read books, talk about books we have all read, eat snacks, hang out," I said with a shrug.

"Fantasy books?" Taylor asked.

I nodded. "Mostly, but sometimes we read other books." I was not about to tell them I read reverse harem books. That would open a can of worms I did not want to deal with. I had made that mistake once.

But, when I thought about it, the book I was currently reading was reverse harem, Tamara knew, and it seemed like the guys knew and didn't care.

"Are you guys free Saturday?" I asked.

"We'll probably be sleeping until the afternoon since we'll be up most of Friday night," Branson said.

Oh, right, the party.

"Well, would you guys want to hang out at the park Saturday afternoon after you wake up?" I suggested.

They looked at each other and gave short nods before facing me again.

"Sure," Taylor said and smiled. "Sounds fun."

"I'll text you guys tonight so you have my number, okay?" I said.

"Okay," Kieran said.

"Bye," I said, turned, and started jogging out of the school.

To my utter surprise, Sean, Wade, and Noah were waiting for me at the corner just down from the school.

I hurried over, smiling wide. "Hey. You guys didn't need to come meet me."

Sean returned my smile. "We wanted to make sure you got home safe."

We started walking, Sean and Wade on my sides and Noah behind me.

"Isn't it safe here?" I asked. Normally small towns were relatively safe.

"Mostly," Sean said and rubbed the back of his neck. "But you're new, so we didn't want to risk you getting scared and running away yet."

"Thanks," I said. "I appreciate it."

"So, I hear you might be interested in joining our gaming sessions?" Sean asked.

I nodded. "I have always wanted to try out the pen and paper games. I just never had anyone to play with."

"I've got a ton of extra dice, so I'll let you have a set," Sean said.

"You still up for working on creating your character tonight?" Noah asked.

I turned around, walking backwards so I could face him. "Yep. You're going to help me, right?"

He smiled and nodded. "All three of us will."

I spun back around. "Sweet."

"What's your favorite type of supernatural creature?" Wade asked.

"Werewolf," I answered immediately. "Well, shapeshifters in general."

"Maybe a shaman then?" Sean asked Noah.

"Maybe."

"I'm not going to the party Friday," I told them.

They looked at each other and then Sean looked down at me. "You're not?"

I shook my head. "I don't want to deal with the drunk people drama."

"Do they know?" Noah asked.

I nodded. "Yep."

"So, do you want to hang out with us then?" Sean asked softly.

"Wasn't that always the plan?" I asked, suddenly feeling nervous. Maybe they had other plans I hadn't known about. "If you're busy, it's okay."

"No, that was the plan," Wade quickly said.

"Cool," I whispered.

"So, do you like playing as a magic user or as a fighter?" Sean asked, steering the conversation back to the game.

"I like using magic," I said with a nod.

"Sorceress then," he said.

"What races are there?" I asked.

The guys began going over the various options, and I allowed myself a moment to enjoy this normal, high school, geek night.

For two hours, they explained the various options in the game and helped me fill out the sheet that they used.

Tamara just kept shaking her head at us, but was also smiling, so I knew she wasn't actually annoyed.

Maybe she was glad I was going to play with them so they wouldn't pester her?

We took a small break while the guys went inside to get more lemonade, so I pulled out my cell phone and sent a text to each of the Gods, just saying hi and it was me.

Once done, I put my phone away and focused on my friends.

I didn't check my phone again until I had eaten dinner, done my homework, and was about to lie down for the night.

Each of them had messaged me twice. I took the time to respond to each of them and wondered about my current life.

There were six guys I was interested in, and it seemed like, were all interested in me.

It was definitely going to be difficult to keep them all straight.

Something hit my window and I walked over, opening it. "Wade, I--" My words stopped as I looked down to find Noah. "Oh, Noah."

He rolled around the other pebbles he had in his hand. "Hey, I just realized I hadn't given you my cell number and wanted to give it to you."

"Oh," I said. "Um, let me just write mine down for you and drop it. That's probably easier in this situation."

He rubbed the back of his neck. "Right."

I quickly wrote my number on a piece of paper, folded it like an airplane, and then let it float down to him.

He chuckled. "Smart. I would have just crumpled it up and dropped it."

I shrugged. "I thought this was more fun."

"Hey, we're okay, right?" he asked as he snagged the paper out of the air.

"Yeah. Why wouldn't we be?"

He shrugged. "I was just worried I'd overstepped your boundaries too much this week. It'll get easier the better we get to know each other."

"Right," I said with a nod.

"Cameron? Who are you talking to?" Mom called through my door.

I made a shooing motion at Noah, closed my curtains, and hopped into my bed just before Mom opened the door and looked inside.

I waved my cell phone at her. "Talking out loud while I text a friend. Sorry."

She came in the room, looked around, and said, "I swore I heard a boy's voice."

I arched a brow at her. "Really, Mom? You think I'd sneak a guy up here? Especially so early? Rude. Super rude."

She patted my arm as she walked out. "Sorry, honey. Night."

"Night, Mom," I called.

I waited until I heard her footsteps go down the stairs before I opened my curtains again, but Noah was gone.

I wasn't sure whether to be sad or not that he was gone.

I was glad that he had come to see me and apologized.

A text came in from an unknown number: *Sorry. I didn't want to get you in trouble. -Noah*

I quickly saved his number before responding to him.

Me: No worries.

Noah: Sunday, do you want to hang out? Just the two of us?

. . .

I stared at my phone. Hang out just the two of us? Wasn't that like a date?

Me: Where?

Noah: We could go to the bakery. Since you aren't going to church, we could go early and be there while everyone else is stuck listening to the sermon... and eat a donut.

Donuts were one of my weaknesses.

Me: Okay. What time?

As we made plans, I wondered if it was really okay. Would the others be mad? Did that matter? I was going to hang out with the Gods Saturday.

I fell asleep with several guys messaging me and a stupid happy smile on my face. Maybe this place wouldn't be so bad after all.

CHAPTER SIX

"You're in a good mood today," Tamara noted.

I shrugged, unable to stop smiling. "Things are good right now."

"Hey," Noah said as he crossed the street to walk with us.

"Morning," I said, smiling at him.

His cheeks grew red, and he looked away from me.

Tamara looked from him to me and she narrowed her eyes. "Oh?"

I shook my head. I was going to have to explain it to her. He was acting like we'd made out or something.

"Hey!" Sean called from the store's door as we passed.

We all waved and called out, "Morning."

"So, is this what small-town life is normally like?" I asked. "Friends greet each other on their way to their everyday tasks and then hang out at night in the fields?"

"That pretty much sums it up," Wade said, panting as he ran to catch us.

"We thought you were going to be out today," Tamara said.

He shook his head. "I just overslept."

"So, we all hanging out tonight?" Tamara asked.

The three of us nodded.

"I'm almost done with the book," I told her.

She squealed. "Thank goodness! I am dying to talk to you about it."

"I have so much to say." I laughed. "So much has happened."

"Isn't it crazy to think about how far they've come from when they first met each other to now?" she asked.

I nodded. "They've been through so much together. Heartache, loss, joy, and victory."

"Who is your favorite?" she asked.

I gaped at her. "You're seriously asking me to choose? That's the whole point of these books, so we don't have to choose."

"Unrealistic expectations," Wade grumbled.

We both looked at him.

"We know this isn't reality," Tamara said softly.

"Yeah, it's just fantasy. We know that. Just like we know we can't shapeshift into a dragon," I said.

He rubbed the back of his neck. "I'm sorry. I didn't mean to upset you two. I know. I'm just grumpy from just waking up, still."

"Well, try to tone it down," Tamara whispered and looked away from him.

We separated to our classes, and I set my hand on her arm. "Hey, he didn't mean anything by it."

She sighed. "I know. I just hate when people do that. I never expected one of them to say that since they like fantasy just like us."

"Yeah, but the type of books we read isn't the same as them. They don't read romances at all, let alone one where the girl can have multiple love interests," I whispered.

"So, that's what you're into?" Branson asked beside me.

I cringed, closed my eyes, and exhaled. Dammit.

"No, it's just one of the many types of stories we read," Tamara said quickly.

I looked at him.

He shrugged. "I'm not judging. I enjoy ridiculous movies where the hero gets all the super hot girls despite being ordinary-looking."

We looked at each other and then at him.

"Please don't try to tell me you think you're ordinary-looking," I said.

He smirked. "So, are you trying to tell me you think I'm attractive?"

I rolled my eyes and pulled out my notebook. "I'm not answering that."

He laughed and nudged me with his elbow. "I'm just teasing you, Cammy."

No one had ever called me that nickname before. I kind of liked it.

"So, we still on for Saturday?" he asked.

I nodded and ignored Tamara's questioning look.

"I hope we didn't keep you up too late last night," he whispered.

Another look from Tamara.

"Branson, shush," I growled.

He looked around me at Tamara and then straightened. "Sorry."

"I thought we were friends," Tamara whisper hissed at me.

I sighed. "Later."

She huffed. "You going to tell me about Noah, too?"

Branson looked over at us.

I let my head drop. "Stop talking," I snapped.

Why were they trying to start drama? Why?

Class ended, and I dragged Tamara to an empty hallway,

looked around, and then quickly and quietly told her everything.

She whistled and smirked. "You go, girl. That's what I'm talking about. You better give me the details sooner though so I know what the heck is going on and I don't give anything away."

I shrugged. "I'm not hiding that I'm talking to them from each other. I'm just not outright telling them. We are only talking as friends right now, but if this weekend's plans are actually dates, then I'm going to have to be upfront with them all."

"And tell them what?" she asked.

"That I'm not looking for a relationship, serious or not, and if they're not okay with me talking to other guys as friends, then they need to tell me that ASAP," I said. "I just want to have friends, and I'd be okay with occasional make out sessions, too."

She laughed loudly, and we headed towards our second period. "I bet you would be."

"We good?" I asked.

She nodded, still smiling wide. "Of course we are. I just want all the details and juice on what's going on. By the way, Sean totally has the hots for you. He's not the best at communicating that type of thing, but I can tell."

I blushed. "What? Really?" All of the time I had spent with him, I had just thought he was being nice. He seemed like a genuinely nice guy, so it surprised me that he might be interested in me.

"Don't get too attached to Sean, Wade, and Noah, though. Those three will be out of this town as soon as they turn eighteen," she whispered.

I shrugged. "That's my goal, too, remember?"

She sighed. "Right. You are all going to leave me alone in

this pathetic little town to sulk in my misery."

"You have choices, too," I whispered.

She shook her head. "I can't get a job, and my family doesn't have anything they could give me. I would be leaving penniless if I did and I don't want to live on the streets in some big town. No thank you, ma'am."

I could totally understand that. If it wasn't for the money my dad had left me when he died, I wouldn't have anything saved either.

"Maybe we can make a plan together."

She waved her hand dismissively. "Don't worry about me. I'm just teasing. I don't mind this town and wouldn't mind just staying here."

"Or maybe a town or two over?" I asked with a smirk.

She elbowed me, and we both started laughing.

At lunch, I felt my phone vibrate in my bag. Careful, so the teachers milling about didn't notice, I pulled it out to read the text message I received.

Kieran: You sure you don't want to come sit with us? Just once.

I glanced over at them, and he smiled shyly at me.

Me: I already told you I don't want to tarnish your reputation.

I looked over, and he made a point of rolling his eyes exaggeratedly. He showed my text to Taylor and Branson who both looked at me and shook their heads.

. . .

Kieran: You're so ridiculous, but fine. Any chance I can call you tonight? Texting is fine and all, but talking is easier.

Me: Sure. 9?

Kieran: It's a date. ;)

"You could just go over there," Noah whispered gruffly beside me.

I put my phone away and looked at him. "I could, but I'd rather eat lunch with you guys."

He wasn't even looking at me, his eyes down on his tray of food.

I pulled out the bag of cookies I'd brought for him, two of Mom's famous chocolate chip cookies, and held it out to him. "Here."

He looked at the bag and then took it. "What's this?"

"Two of my mom's cookies. I thought you might like them, since you eat the crap food here all the time, I wanted to give you something yummy to eat."

He smiled, and I felt butterflies in my stomach. "Thanks, Cam."

I nodded and turned away, packing up my bag to get ready for class. "You're welcome."

"How come I didn't get cookies?" Wade pouted.

"I'll bring you some next time," I promised.

He smiled. "Sweet."

"So, tonight, do I still just come over right after school?" I asked.

Tamara nodded. "Yep."

"Don't your parents get irritated with feeding us all the time?" I asked softly.

She laughed. "No. She would feed every kid in this town if

it meant ensuring I was home and not out doing drugs or foolin' around."

I laughed. "I guess that makes sense."

"You keep inflating her ego and she'll be unbearable though. She tried to make me call her Goddess this morning." Tamara shook her head. "Crazy woman."

I laughed. "I'll call her it tonight."

Tamara groaned. "I swear. You are just trying to make me look bad to my own mama."

I shrugged. "Don't get mad at me if she likes me better."

Wade scoffed. "Please, we all know that I'm her favorite."

Tamara rolled her eyes. "You were her favorite when we were six. Now you're a teenage boy and she goes back and forth between wanting to smack you and wanting to feed you."

"Why would she smack me? I'm a perfectly behaved gentleman," he said, sat straighter, and pretended to adjust a tie.

We all laughed.

"What?" he asked with a scowl.

"You are something alright, but it isn't a gentleman," Noah said and shook his head.

"Special," Tamara said and scoffed. "Super special."

"You two are just jealous," he said and shoveled a huge spoonful of grits into his mouth. "Jealous," he said around the mouthful.

I gagged. "Such great manners."

Tamara and Noah laughed.

Wade blushed. "Sorry," he said after he swallowed.

Noah took out one of his cookies, and I snatched it, grabbing a piece and handed it to Wade.

"Hey!" Noah complained.

Wade took it with a huge smile, looking like a little kid

with a present. He popped it in his mouth and then chewed on it slowly, savoring the flavor. "So good."

"That was my piece," Noah muttered and shoved the rest of the cookie into his mouth.

Why? Why was I warming up to these people so quickly? I had avoided others like the plague after all of the crap I had been through and yet here I was making friends quickly with these people.

Noah set his hand on my forearm. "Hey, you okay?"

I jerked away from him and then exhaled and nodded. "Yeah, sorry."

"Do you bake?" Wade asked.

I shook my head, happy for the change of topic. "No, I burn everything. Mom keeps trying to get me into the kitchen, but I suck at baking."

"Maybe you're better at cooking meals than baking," Tamara said. "I know some people are like that."

I shrugged. "Maybe, but I refuse to let my mom groom me for a stay-at-home-wife life. I don't want to do that. I have goals. Plans. Ambitions."

"Like what?" Noah asked.

"I want to become a veterinarian," I whispered. That wasn't something I had told anyone since elementary school.

"Our vet is super cool," Wade said and smiled. "She's really nice and explains everything so you can understand what is really going on with your animal."

"I don't have pets, but I'd like to meet her," I whispered.

"She's my sister, so I can arrange that," Noah said.

My eyes widened, and I turned to face him. "Really?"

He smiled. "Sure. If you want to come over on Thursday evening, you can meet her. She stays for family dinner that night."

I blushed. "I don't want to intrude on family dinner night."

He scoffed. "Trust me, my parents would be ecstatic to have me bring a girl over, even a friend."

I touched my purple hair. "You sure?"

He leaned over and said, "I'm positive."

"Moving a little fast, aren't you?" Wade asked Noah with a scowl.

Noah rolled his eyes. "She's coming over to talk to my sister. That's hardly moving fast."

"Rules," Wade snapped.

"What rules?" Tamara asked.

Wade and Noah were suddenly really focused on their food trays despite the fact that they were both mostly empty.

Interesting.

"Hey, tomorrow, do you want to do our nails?" Tamara asked me.

"In the evening?" I asked back.

She nodded.

"Sure. I haven't had someone paint my nails in a really long time. That would be nice," I said.

"I only have three colors because the stores here don't offer a very wide selection," she said softly.

"I can try to get more from the next town," Noah offered.

"We should make a group trip," Tamara said with shiny eyes.

I narrowed my eyes at her, suspecting she just wanted to go see the guy she was crushing on. "Hm."

"Cam hasn't seen the other towns," she added. "We should show her around."

"It would be fun to get out," Wade said and shrugged. "I'm game."

"We'll have to talk to Sean," Noah said. "But I doubt he will say no."

"Let's have Cam ask," Tamara said. "He won't say no to her."

I glared at her. "I don't like what you are insinuating."

She smirked, but said nothing else.

"Please?" Wade asked.

I sighed and let my head drop. "Okay, but when are we going to go?"

"Sunday afternoon?" Wade suggested.

Tamara nodded. "After church."

"Works for me," Noah said, glanced at me, and then returned to eating the food on his tray.

"Okay," I agreed. "I will ask Sean."

"Woohoo!" Tamara whooped and threw a fist into the air.

"If he says no, you can't blame me," I muttered.

"He won't say no to you," Noah whispered.

I didn't respond, letting the topic drop.

I was quiet through the rest of the school day, trying to figure out how I had let myself become so embroiled in a group's dynamic when all I had wanted to do was blend into the background.

"You okay?" Tamara asked as we headed from the school towards the store where Sean worked.

I nodded. "Yep."

"Are we overwhelming you?" she asked softly. "Mama said you dealt with a lot at your previous schools."

I smiled and slung my arm across her shoulders like she had done so many times to me. "You're good. Just realizing that things are not going the way I had planned, but I'm not sure I actually care that they aren't going the way I had planned."

"If we make you uncomfortable, please let us know," she whispered.

I nodded. "Will do."

We entered Sean's shop, and I hurried to the fiction section.

"We don't have any new books," Sean said softly behind me.

"Are you going this weekend to find more?" I asked without turning around.

"Yes."

"Next weekend, will you take me with you?" I requested.

"Sure," he said. "I'd like to spend more time with you."

"Sean?"

"Yeah?"

I turned around and smiled at him. "Thank you for making me feel so welcomed here."

He smiled back. "You are welcome. I only wish I could make you feel more at ease in the evenings."

I laughed. "I'll get there. I'm just not used to being around people I can trust. Yet."

He reached past me and picked up a book from the shelf. "You will probably enjoy this one."

I took it and read the blurb on the back. It sounded really interesting.

I held out two dollars, paying for this book and the extra I owed him. "Here." He took it and tried to give me the change, but I left the store with a wave. "See you later."

That night, as we sat on Tamara's back porch, Sean slid something into my backpack.

"What is that?" I asked, closing my book.

He pushed my book back towards me. "Nothing. Read your book."

I glared at him, but resumed reading my book, finally getting to the ending so I could talk about it with Tamara.

"Oh, my goodness!" I screeched at her.

She nodded. "I know, right?"

"So much. There was so much that happened."

She nodded again. "Right? They went from just meeting to a fully-fledged family."

"I want to know what happens next," I said.

She shook her head. "The writer said she won't write more in that series. That it is complete with just those two books."

I groaned. "I know she left it open-ended, but there is still so much that could happen."

She nodded. "I know."

We both sighed, and I let my head droop.

"Don't you have something to ask?" Tamara asked me and tilted her head towards Sean.

Oh, right.

I turned to Sean, certain I was blushing. "I know I asked if I could go with you next weekend to find more books. However, I was wondering if you might go this Sunday afternoon and let everyone come so we could make a group trip of it?"

He smiled and nodded. "Sure. I bet you would like to see more of the nearby towns and get a feel for the true atmosphere of our area."

"Woohoo!" Tamara cheered. "Road trip."

I narrowed my eyes at her, but she just smiled smugly.

"Thank you," I whispered to Sean.

He leaned closer to me and whispered, "If you'd like to go without the others sometime, I'm up for that as well. I'd love to show you around."

"Thanks," I whispered and smiled at him. "I might take you up on that offer soon."

He nodded. "The offer is always open." He leaned closer and whispered, "And if you don't feel comfortable going with just me in the future, you can just tell me."

My eyes widened, my mouth dropped, and I shook my head. "No. No. That wasn't it. I just—"

He smiled, warmth filling his eyes unlike anything I had seen from friends at my previous schools. "It's okay. Just wanted you to know I won't take offense. Okay?"

I closed my mouth, swallowed hard, and nodded. Was I screwing things up already?

"So, we all road-tripping Sunday?" Wade asked.

"Road trip!" Sean exclaimed

Everyone cheered.

"What time do you usually leave?" I asked, remembering Noah and I had a breakfast date.

"Right after church," Sean said. "So, about noon. Does that work for you?"

I nodded and took a big drink of lemonade. "Perfect."

Noah glanced at me and then smirked as he returned to reading his book.

Tamara noticed and gave me a grin and waggled her eyebrows.

Had I not been overly careful with my books, I would have thrown mine at her. Instead, I just gave her my best glare and rolled my eyes.

CHAPTER SEVEN

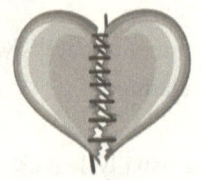

At exactly nine o'clock, I received a text message from Kieran.

Kieran: You still awake?
  Me: Yes. Finishing math homework. What are you up to?
  Kieran: Need help? I finished it earlier.

That was definitely the first time I had ever received an offer for math help from a guy. I was more surprised that he had finished it as well, since it was Friday night and we had the weekend to finish it.

Me: Thanks, but I'll be done in just a minute or two.
  Kieran: Want me to wait until you're done to talk?
  Me: No. It's okay. What's up?
  Kieran: How are you liking our school?
  Me: It's different than others, but I enjoy it.

· · ·

It showed him typing for a long time, so I was surprised when the response was so short.

Kieran: Can I call? It's easier than typing this all out. LOL.
  Me: Sure. Give me one minute to finish up my last math problem.
  Kieran: K

I hurried to finish up my last problem, put my book and binder in my backpack, shut my bedroom door, and then turned on music. Mom wouldn't care that I was making friends, even with a boy, but that didn't mean I wanted her to eavesdrop.

She might have been my mother, but she was a gossiper and the entire church would know every word I said by nine o'clock tomorrow morning if I let her hear.

My phone rang, and I got a jolt of excitement that made my heart race.

Why did I react like this with these boys? Why was I reacting this way with *so many* different boys?

"Hello?" I answered, like I didn't have caller ID and didn't know it was him.

"Hey," Kieran said, his deep voice soft and sultry.

"What's up?" I asked.

"You finish your homework?"

I nodded, then realized he couldn't see that. "Yep."

"Hey, put her on speaker phone," Branson said in the background.

"Go to your own house, dammit," Kieran said. "I didn't ask her to talk to all of us."

"Stop being stingy and share," Branson grumbled.

I laughed.

"Come on, just ask her if she wouldn't mind being on speaker and talking to all of us," Taylor said.

"I don't mind," I answered before he could ask.

Kieran sighed. "Next time I'm going to leave and go to one of your house's so I can have some privacy."

"You guys hang out together often?" I asked.

"Yep!" Branson chirped.

"I can't get rid of them," Kieran grumbled.

"So, Cam, what have you been up to tonight?" Taylor asked.

"Hung out at Tamara's before coming in for dinner and then doing my homework," I answered.

"You hang out with her often?" Branson asked.

"Her and her friends, each evening so far," I answered.

"Her friends? Not your friends?" Taylor asked.

I supposed they were my friends, but I'd only known them a week.

"I think it's a bit early to claim them as friends," I answered softly.

"Does that mean you don't consider us friends?" Branson asked. "Ouch, my feelings are hurt."

I rolled my eyes. "Seeing as we've hardly spoken, no I don't."

"Yet," Taylor added. "You don't... yet."

"I don't make friends easily," I warned them. "I've been stabbed in the back too many times for that."

"Friends protect your back, not stab it," Kieran said.

"Want us to stab those people back for you?" Branson asked in a super excited voice.

"I'd rather no one stabbed anyone," I whispered.

There was silence on the line a moment.

"I was just joking," Branson said. "I wouldn't hurt a fly."

"The big dope couldn't hurt someone if he tried," Taylor said.

"So, you're not too keen on friends," Kieran said. "What else should we know about you?"

"Are you a hugger?" Taylor asked.

Tears brimmed in my eyes as I thought about trying to explain my PTSD and the events that caused it.

"At times," I whispered.

"Noted. So, Branson, keep your hands to yourself," Kieran said sternly.

"Okay," Branson said softly.

"Wait!" I gasped. "Isn't tonight that party you all are supposed to go to?"

"Oh, so you did remember it was happening?" Taylor asked.

"Yeah, but I'm not going," I mumbled.

"Why not?"

"Reasons. So, why aren't you there?" I asked.

"Well, we were actually hoping to convince you to come out tonight," Branson said.

I opened my mouth, but before I could say anything Kieran interrupted.

"Not to the party, but just to hang out with us, outside your house," he said.

"We're meeting tomorrow, remember?" I whispered and looked out my window at the pitch-black sky.

"What time?" Taylor asked.

"We said the afternoon so you would have time to wake up after the party," I reminded them.

"You sure you won't come out tonight?" Branson asked and I could picture him pouting.

"Sorry, not this time," I said.

"We've got to earn her trust first," Taylor said softly. "I wouldn't want to go outside in the dark with you two if I didn't know you either."

"Us? You're the scary-looking one," Branson said with a scoff.

"What's your favorite flower?" Kieran asked.

The question caught me so off guard that I didn't respond for a long moment.

"Uh, tulips," I said.

"Oh, I'm more of a sunflower man," Branson said.

"Sunflowers, huh?" I asked, smirking. "What about you Taylor?"

"I like roses. Red roses," Taylor said.

"Kieran?" I asked.

"You'll have to wait and find out tomorrow when we hang out," he said.

"Tease," I said.

"He's such a tease," Branson agreed.

"What are your favorite chips?" I asked.

"Sour Cream & Onion," Branson said immediately.

"Barbecue," Taylor said.

"Tortilla chips and salsa," Kieran said.

"You?" Branson asked.

"You'll have to wait until tomorrow," I said.

All three groaned, which made me laugh.

"Eleven tomorrow?" Taylor asked.

"Okay. What should I bring?"

"Just your beautiful self," Branson said. "We'll bring snacks."

"You're not allergic to anything, right?" Taylor asked.

"Bad attitudes," I said.

"Well, I'm not coming then," Kieran said.

I laughed a bit too loud and heard my mom coming to investigate. "Got to go, boys. See you tomorrow."

"Eleven," Kieran said.

"Eleven," I agreed.

"Bye!" Taylor and Branson yelled.

I hung up the phone right as Mom opened the door. "What was that?" she asked.

I blinked. "Me laughing?"

She blinked back. "Oh."

"Did I wake you?"

She shook her head. "No, I just wanted to check on you."

I smiled. "Thanks. I'm good."

She looked at me a long moment and said, "I think you are. Much better, actually. Good night, Cameron."

"Night, Mom."

Despite saying good night, I couldn't sleep, but for once it wasn't nerves of fear or anxiety. It was excitement coursing through me.

I kept reminding myself I didn't know these guys and the last time I had let myself trust too quickly bad things had happened.

Yet, I was still excited for tomorrow. We would be in broad daylight, in a public park, and I knew Tamara was planning on passing by about an hour into the date. So, it was as safe as I could make it.

Safer than ninety percent of my other dates and only a couple of those had gone bad.

At some point I fell asleep, but when I woke up and looked at the clock to see 10:45 AM, I screeched before leaping out of bed.

"What's wrong?" Mom called up to me.

"I forgot to set an alarm, and I made lunch plans with friends!" I yelled down as I rushed to get changed.

"You need food?" she asked.

"Just a small snack," I called back down.

Jeans and t-shirt on, I ran into the bathroom to brush out my hair and put on minimal makeup.

My hair was still a bright purple, which made me incredibly happy.

Finally satisfied with my appearance, I ran down the stairs and put my shoes on.

"Here," Mom said and handed me a half sandwich with scrambled eggs and cheese.

I kissed her cheek. "You're the best mama ever."

She smirked. "You know it."

I waved back to her as she watched me run out of the house, shoving the sandwich in my mouth.

I knew the guys were bringing food, but I didn't want to gorge myself on their food. I didn't want them to think I was a pig on the first time we hung out.

I jogged across town, waving at Sean as I passed the store where he was inside helping a customer.

He waved back, smiling wide.

Finally, I made it to the park, which was really just yet another rural part that they added a metal jungle gym and slide to, some swings, a few park benches, and a water fountain.

I expected to be the first one there, even though I was exactly on time, but all three guys sat on a blanket on the grass under a tree with snacks in the center of the blanket.

Whoa.

"Hey!" Branson called out and waved, smiling.

I waved back and walked over, trying to get my breathing back to a normal range as well as my heartbeat. I didn't want them knowing I ran here. That would be embarrassing.

"Morning," I said as I stood before them.

They had left the bottom of the square blanket open, but I didn't want to sit without knowing for sure where I was welcomed.

"Sit," Taylor said and waved at the open spot.

"Have any trouble finding the place?" Kieran asked.

I chuckled. "Super hard to find. I ran across the entire town to find it."

All three laughed, and I relaxed on the blanket.

These three were large guys, at least six feet tall and muscular, but when I sat with them, I felt safe instead of nervous. I'd been around some large guys at my last school that were truly frightening. Then again, those guys had been part of gangs whereas these guys had probably never even seen a gang member.

"Were you waiting long?" I asked.

"All night," Kieran teased with a smirk.

"So, you three best friends in more ways than one?" I asked.

"Of course someone from California would ask that," Taylor said and rolled his eyes.

I shrugged. "It's an honest question. No need to be embarrassed. I had several gay friends and had a girlfriend or two before. I'm not judging, just trying to understand you better."

"No, we aren't lovers," Kieran said matter-of-factly.

"Then why are you single? You've got girls throwing themselves at you. Kar...Sylvia even went as far as to threaten me."

"She did what?" Kieran asked, his shoulders rigid, and his hands clenching into fists.

I waved at him. "Don't worry about it. I explained that I told you guys to go after her. Plus, I can handle girls like her."

"She's annoying as a mosquito," Branson said. "Acts like she has some divine right to us. No, thank you."

"She's pretty," I said and shrugged. "You could do worse."

Kieran looked at me. "If you try to suggest that she is prettier than you, I will throw up on our snacks."

I clamped my lips together to keep from saying anything and to hide my smile.

Taylor groaned. "You're serious? Or is this just you looking for a compliment."

My brows furrowed, and I glared at him. "Wow. I know we don't know each other that well, but that's just freaking rude."

He smiled and I realized he had done it to get a rise out of me. Wow.

I leaned back and exhaled.

"What kind of drink do you want?" Taylor asked, pointing at the soda cans.

I grabbed my favorite and opened it. "Thanks for bringing snacks," I said.

"Grab whatever you want. We share everything," Branson said.

That statement had me wondering dirty things, and I wondered if I blushed.

"Would you mind telling us some of what happened to make you move all the way out here to BFE?" Kieran asked softly like he was afraid I might run off.

I grabbed a chip and chewed it up before asking, "Are you sure you want to hear? It's going to change how you view me and I've only had a week here. You might end up not wanting to even talk to me."

Branson rolled his eyes and smiled. "That's not going to happen, Cam."

They didn't know that. Not for certain.

Maybe it would be good to get it out in the open with them and then when they stopped talking to me, it would leave me time to focus on finding people who would want to be around me even after learning my past. I wasn't even worried about them spreading it around the school, honestly.

"Promise me one thing?" I asked.

They all nodded.

"If you decide you don't want to talk to me, just don't be

rude at school? Just ignore me, okay? Don't say snide comments or rude things. I can handle you ignoring me, but the snide comments start wearing on a person after a while."

"We wouldn't—" Branson started, but Kieran held his hand up.

"We promise we will not use what you tell us as ammunition to make rude comments and if we do not wish to speak to you or associate with you, will act as if you do not exist instead," Kieran said.

Taylor and Branson scowled, looking at each other for a long moment before they repeated the same thing.

Why did it hurt to hear Kieran say he would act as though I didn't exist?

Why were tears threatening to fall just at the suggestion?

I dropped my head and wiped my eyes.

"Cam?" Taylor asked.

"Can I give the abridged explanation?" I asked, sniffling.

"Yeah, whatever you are comfortable with," Branson said.

I grabbed a chip and ate it before speaking. The words tumbled out of my mouth faster than I intended them to. "I went to a pretty bad school. Lots of fights, shootings, stabbings, and drugs. There were gangs, and I got mixed up in one. I wasn't part of the gang, but interacted with them a lot. I had a few friends I spent a lot of time with. Bad kids who were always drinking and doing drugs. I got in several fights with them and then one night, they decided that since I wasn't part of the gang, they would use me as bait."

My breath caught, and I looked up at the sky, letting the sun warm my face to remind me I wasn't there.

"Cam, you don't—" Branson started, but I shook my head.

"They took me back to the house they were squatting in, got me higher than I'd ever been before, beat the shit out of me, and then dumped me on the front lawn of the school."

I took a shuddering breath, and Taylor reached out towards me, but then dropped his hand. "You survived, though," he said softly.

I laughed mirthlessly. "Yeah. I lived. But then my friends, if you could call them that, wouldn't talk to me because the other gang had shown how weak I was. That night I tried to end my life, but Mom found me and the paramedics arrived and saved me."

"You tried to kill yourself?" Branson asked.

I nodded, unable to speak.

Kieran stood, brushed off his jeans, and then held out a hand to me.

I thought he was going to ask me to leave, so I accepted his hand, preparing to leave, tears already streaming down my face.

Instead, he pulled me into his arms and held me.

I rested my face against his shirt, well aware I was soaking it with my tears and snot, but he'd offered.

Branson hugged me from the right side, hugging Kieran, too.

Then Taylor joined, hugging me from the left.

I had never been hugged by three guys at once, and it was honestly really reassuring.

"I'm sorry," I whispered. "I didn't think I'd cry like this again."

"Shush," Kieran ordered me.

I stopped talking and let them hold me and before long, I actually felt a sense of relief and comfort wash over me.

"You had a lot of messed up things happen to you. You had people use you and treat you like trash. I get it now, why you view yourself so poorly. I don't understand it, I won't ever claim to understand what you went through. However, we are here and we aren't going to stop trying to be your friend because of your past," Kieran whispered in my ear.

"What he said," Taylor whispered.

"Yeah," Branson said. "We're not assholes. Well, not most of the time."

"We better separate before the town spreads rumors about us fornicating on the grass," I said with a chuckle.

They released me and before I could wipe my eyes, Kieran did it for me, making me look up at him.

"Thank you," I whispered to him.

Even if this was just a ploy to get me to sleep with them, it made me feel better.

He nodded once, sat down, and then waited for me to do the same.

CHAPTER EIGHT

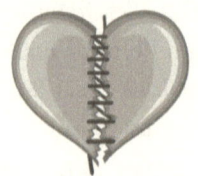

Having told the Gods about my life, and feeling their acceptance, made me realize I needed to do the same with Tamara and her friends.

If they wouldn't accept me, I needed to know now.

But it wasn't a topic I just wanted to bring up and spring on them.

So, how to do it?

After I'd told them, the trio of Gods had spent the rest of our time together telling me funny stories and making me laugh until I cried.

It was nice to cry for a different reason.

I'd left with a hug from each and a bit of hope in my heart that maybe, just maybe, I could move on with my life in a positive way.

That there were others out there who wouldn't treat me as poorly as those in California had.

"Hey," Noah greeted me, standing from the booth in the donut shop where he'd been sitting.

I smiled and waved. "Hey."

We sat on opposite sides of the booth and an older man with an apron came over. "Ready to order?"

I glanced at the menu, but quickly set it down. "Noah, can you order something for me?"

He smiled, nodded, and placed an order while I looked around the cute café. There was only one other patron, an old man bent over a cup of coffee at the counter.

"Everyone else is at church," Noah said. "It's the perfect time to come here."

I had to agree. Coming when it was empty like this was perfect. "It's nice," I said.

"So, you excited for our trip later today?" he asked.

I nodded, beaming. "Super excited. I hope we find some good books."

He chuckled. "You look just like Sean right now. He's always more excited for the books than the trip, too."

My cheeks warmed. "I'm excited for the trip."

"Here's your cocoa," the old man in the apron said and set the steaming mugs in front of us.

"Thank you," I said and smiled up at him.

He nodded and hobbled off.

"That's Sam," Noah told me. "He's owned this shop for forty years. He and his wife opened it together."

"Where's his wife?" I asked.

"Cooking," Noah answered immediately. "Sharon makes the best donuts ever."

"Damn straight I do," an old woman in a blue and white striped dress with curly grey hair and bright blue eyes said as she walked out to us with a plate of four donuts on it. "And if you don't agree, your taste buds are broken."

I chuckled. I liked her already.

After one bite of the chocolate glazed donut, I moaned and

my eyes rolled into the back of my head. "Oh my. That's...heaven."

She chuckled. "She's a keeper, Noah. I like her. You can come in here whenever you want..."

"Cam," I said, opened my eyes and held out my hand. "My Mama and I just moved here."

She shook my hand. "Nice to meet you, Cam. Love the hair."

I touched it and smiled. "Thank you, ma'am."

"I dyed my hair pink once, wasn't on purpose mind you, but Sam loved it. Tried to convince me to keep it, but the town was in a tizzy over it for a month. I changed it back so I wouldn't have to keep hearing about all the sins I was bound to make," Sharon said.

"You should do it again," I told her. "I think pink would go lovely with your skin tone."

She touched her curls. "Maybe I will. At my age, what's the worst they could say?"

I smiled, and she smiled back at me, two troublemakers in one room.

"Alright, Sharon, can we have some privacy?" Noah asked.

She scoffed. "Boy, you are lucky I like you."

"You love me and you know it," Noah teased with a wink.

She laughed and walked back to the kitchens.

"Come here often?" I asked.

He shrugged. "Not many other places to go on Sunday. They've never been religious, so they kept their shop open even though they only get one or two customers this time. They said it was those one or two customers who mattered the most. They were the most underserved."

They weren't wrong and that type of attitude is what made lifelong patrons out of people.

"Guess I know my new Sunday breakfast spot," I said with a smile.

"Good to know," Kieran said as he approached the counter.

Noah's eyes narrowed as mine widened.

"Kieran, what are you doing here?" I asked.

"Just getting some donuts to go," he said with a scowl. "Don't let me interrupt your date."

"We won't," Noah said with a scowl.

"Easy," I whispered. "We're friends, remember?"

His scowl didn't lessen.

Boys were so much trouble.

"See you tomorrow," Kieran said, bent, and kissed my cheek on his way out.

Noah's jaw clenched, and he looked down at the table.

Dammit. Why? Why had I not expected something like this?

"Don't mind him," I whispered. "He's just happy I opened up to him and his friends yesterday."

Noah raised his head. "What do you mean?"

"Well, I wanted to tell you and the others, but I'm not sure when is exactly a good time to bring it up since it's not an easy topic to discuss."

"You mean about your past?" he asked.

I nodded and took a sip of my hot chocolate. Perfect chocolate-y goodness.

"I'd like to hear that, but this is definitely not the right place. How about tonight after our trip?" he suggested.

I nodded again. "Okay."

We ate the rest of the donuts in silence and then made our way to Tamara's house to wait for everyone else to come.

"Cam?" Noah asked from the seat beside me.

"Hm?" I asked, looking up from the new book I was reading.

"Can I sit next to you?" he asked.

I smirked and nodded. "Sure."

He moved to join me on the love seat, sitting so close that our thighs touched from hip to knee.

I tried to focus back on reading, but no matter how many times I read the page I was on, I couldn't comprehend it.

Finally, after what felt like an hour, Tamara, Wade, and Sean arrived.

"Ready?" Sean asked me.

I hopped up, smiling wide. "You know it!"

"Road trip!" Tamara yelled.

"Y'all better behave," Tamara's mom snapped from inside the house.

"Don't worry, mighty Goddess. I shall keep everyone in eyesight and ensure nothing bad happens," I called inside.

She chuckled. "You better or this goddess will give you a mighty whoopin'."

"Understood!" I called back and hurried Tamara out to the front of the house where Sean's SUV waited.

"Kiss ass," Tamara mumbled.

We climbed into the waiting car and buckled in. Noah sat in the front passenger seat while Wade sat beside me and Tamara.

"Road trip!" Wade yelled.

I chuckled and then yelled, "Road trip!"

Sean looked at me in the rearview mirror and winked once before starting the vehicle and heading out of our small town.

I watched the scenery out the window, wondering what others thought of living in such a rural location. We had one fire station, one police station, and one hospital that was fifteen minutes away.

Everything had been so close in my previous home that I had taken it for granted. I never had to worry if we would make it to the hospital in time or if the fire department would make it in time to extinguish a fire in my house.

Here though, that was a definite fear.

"You're scowling," Tamara whispered. "What are you thinking about?"

"You guys ever worry about fires or having to race to a hospital?" I asked, glancing at everyone in the SUV.

They all shrugged.

"Not really," Tamara said. "The sheriff and deputy are trained in first aid and most of the town is, actually. And the fire department are pretty fast to respond, but we help each other out."

Seemed strange to me, but I could understand it if I looked at it from their points of view. This was what they were used to. Nothing about this seemed strange to someone who was raised with this as the normal.

"You seem really nervous about it," Wade commented.

"We had services really close, so this is abnormal to me," I explained.

"It's part of why the boys aren't as crazy as they could be," Tamara said. "They know if they severely injure themselves, they'll have to ride in a bumpy ambulance for a long time before actually being seen by a doctor."

"Or, it's because we're smart enough not to do stupid things," Noah said.

"I think Tamara's right," I said with a smirk.

Noah looked at me and then smiled and laughed while shaking his head. "Of course you do."

"Here we are!" Sean exclaimed as he turned onto a dirt road with no signs.

"Uh, where is here?" I asked, looking at trees as far as I could see.

"Just give it a minute," Sean said.

Skepticism in place, I waited as we bounced down the dirt road. Two minutes later, we emerged from the trees to a town similar to ours, but hidden amongst the trees.

"Whoa," I whispered.

Every building was built out of logs and there were easily twice as many people here as our town.

Sean drove through the town slowly, stopping several times for pedestrians crossing the street and then parked in a small lot.

We all climbed out, and they led me away from the parking lot, past several shops, and to a huge grassy area filled with pop up tents where people were selling their items.

"It's a huge garage sale," I whispered.

Sean nodded. "It's a rummage sale," he explained. "They let the entire town come so people don't have to try to drive down twisty dirt roads for each house. It's a lot easier for selling their items and for outsiders to find them."

I jogged so I was beside Sean and smiled up at him. "You're practically glowing with excitement," I told him.

He blushed and rubbed the back of his neck. "I like these types of things. My mom used to bring me here when I was little and it became something we did every weekend."

The way he talked about her in past tense was a dead giveaway.

"Maybe it can be our thing for the year," I suggested.

He looked down at me and nodded. "I'd like that."

We joined the group of people walking down the rows of merchants, and I felt like an adventurer looking for wares.

A huge group jostled us around, and Sean reached out, taking my hand with his, interlacing our fingers, and continued forward.

My cheeks warmed, and I looked down at my shoes to hide the blush.

Behind me, someone grabbed my hand, and I turned to find Noah holding my other hand.

Two boys holding my hands. The people who saw us were likely praying and sputtering about the whore in their midst.

"Oh," Sean said and stopped.

Instantly, he released my hand, and I felt cold without his warm hand holding mine.

I looked at the place we had stopped at and was disappointed to see mostly religious books. It made sense that Sean would want to stop here, since they would do well in his shop, but they didn't interest me.

Noah tugged on my hand, and I let him pull me across the way to another person who had several board games and a few fantasy novels for sale.

"Oh," I said, released his hand, and knelt to examine the books.

"You like books," the older woman asked as she fanned herself with a folded piece of paper.

I nodded and smiled up at her. "I do."

She stood slowly, hobbled to a plastic tub behind her, and pulled the lid off. "These might interest you then."

I walked over, glanced inside and squealed.

Several people turned to look at us and I flushed with embarrassment.

The woman chuckled. "I'll sell the lot to you for five dollars."

I gaped at her. "You can't be serious."

She nodded. "They were my late husband's and he just wanted someone to enjoy them. I can tell that you would enjoy these as much as he did."

I fished out a five-dollar bill, handed it to her, and then chewed on my lip. "Could I leave it all here until we're done doing the rest of our shopping?"

She nodded, stuffed the bill into her bra, and said, "I'll keep them safe for you. Don't worry, honey."

"Thank you," I said and stroked the book on the top, one of my favorite fantasy books ever, before letting her put the lid back on.

"Did you just snag the best haul ever?" Sean asked.

I spun around and chewed on my lower lip. "Sorry."

He smiled. "Don't be sorry. Just let me borrow them."

I nodded vigorously. "Whichever one you want!"

He glanced at my lips and then turned away. "Let's go check out the rest of the sellers."

"Oh," Tamara whispered as she came up behind me. "You got him frazzled. I've never seen him so worked up."

I rolled my eyes at her. "Whatever."

We started walking, and I ran into a guy almost immediately upon entering back into the crowd.

"I'm so sorry," I said as I rubbed at my sore chest from the ground where I'd fallen.

The guy looked down at me, well over six feet tall, muscular, and homely. His nose was a bit too large for his face and he had one eye slightly lower than the other. "I'm sorry," he said. He held out his hand, and I let him help me stand.

"You okay?" Tamara asked me.

I nodded and dusted off my butt. "Sorry, man. I didn't see you."

"Totally my fault," he said. "Hey, um, this might seem weird, but could I have your number?"

I flinched and Tamara noticed, putting her hand on my lower back.

"Sorry, I appreciate the compliment, but I don't give out my number," I whispered.

"Are you from here? I don't recognize you, so you must be

from one of the nearby towns," he said, taking a step closer to me.

I took a step back, feeling like he was towering over me.

"Um...I..." I licked my lips, feeling scared and unsafe despite being surrounded by people and with Tamara at my back.

"There you are," Branson said as he forced his way through people to get to me, pushing the guy in front of me back a step so he could drape an arm across my shoulders. "You're so short I lost sight of you." He winked down at me, and I immediately exhaled in relief.

"Stop running off," Kieran scolded me as he came up on my other side, pushing Branson's arm off and linking our hands together, pulling me a step farther away from the guy.

"Sorry," I mumbled.

Tamara's eyes were wide as saucers as she looked at the guy and then at the Gods with us.

"Can we help you?" Taylor asked from behind the guy.

"Are you dating them?" the guy asked.

"No, but—" I started.

"It's not any of your business," Kieran said with a glare. "Come on, Cam—"

"I wasn't talking to you," the guy said sternly.

Kieran's eyes darkened as he raised them to meet the guy. "Piss off."

"Hey," I said, stepping away from Kieran. "Let's all just calm down."

"You seem awfully chatty for someone who isn't her boyfriend," the guy said. "I suppose that means you want to be hers, but you aren't yet."

"Cam?" Noah called, pushing through to reach us. He looked around at all the tense guys and scowled. "What's going on?"

Sean pushed through, took a look around, and held his hand out to me. "Come on."

I took his hand, mine shaking majorly, and Tamara took my other hand, hers shaking, too.

Sean pulled us into the crowd and away from the testosterone insanity. "You okay?" he asked me.

I nodded, staring at my feet as he led us away.

"I'm not!" Tamara shouted. "What the hell was up with all of that?"

"He's not a nice person," Sean said softly. "I've had a few run-ins with him and none were pleasant. Let's keep you away from him."

"Yes, please," I whispered.

Sean squeezed my hand, but it felt like an involuntary reaction.

"What are the Gods doing here?" Tamara asked me.

I looked over my shoulder at her and shrugged.

As I looked, behind her I saw Kieran standing face to face with the guy, neither looking happy.

"I don't want them to fight," I said.

"Don't worry, they won't," Sean said. "Kieran is really good at making people back down."

"What?" I asked.

He shrugged. "It's like the opposite of someone who can make everyone calm down. He makes everyone nervous and not want to fight anymore."

"That is super weird," I said.

"He's a decent guy," Sean said softly. "I think it's just that alpha-ish aura he has. You know if you fight him that you better be ready to go all out because he isn't going to let you stop once it starts."

"I would love to see him fight," Tamara said breathlessly behind us.

Sean stopped in front of a booth with walls, carpet on the ground, and two teenagers running it. "Hey!" he greeted them and released my hand.

I stumbled, feeling the loss of his touch like a lifeline.

"You okay?" Tamara asked.

"Does he affect everyone so much?" I asked mostly to myself.

"Yeah, he makes you feel super safe," she said. "And when you separate it's like you're free floating a moment, right?"

I nodded, surprised she felt that same way.

"I don't know how to explain it logically, but I feel that with him, too," she said. "And I have absolutely zero interest in him as anything other than a friend."

So, it wasn't just because I was attracted to him then. Good to know.

"Hey, boo," a deep male voice called.

I turned and my jaw dropped at the dark god before us.

Tamara chuckled softly and lightly punched my arm. "He's mine, bitch. Back down."

"Yours? What?" I asked, but my question was answered when she stepped forward and he hugged her and kissed her.

This was her boyfriend in the other city.

Damn, homegirl knew how to pick them. He was tall, muscular, dark, and hot as Hades.

"Hey," Kieran said behind me.

I spun around and immediately checked him for injuries. "What happened? Please tell me you didn't fight that guy because of me."

He pulled me into his chest and hugged me. "Calm down, Cam. I'm fine. I didn't fight him. I really wanted to punch the bastard, but I didn't. It's okay. I got him to back down and leave. Are you okay?"

I shouldn't have been fine with this person I barely knew

hugging me and yet I melted against him and teared up a little bit.

I sniffled and wiped my face on his shirt. "I'm fine."

"Liar," he whispered.

I looked up at him, and he wiped my face with his thumbs. "If he gives you anymore trouble, you yell for us, okay?"

"What?" I asked, confused by this closeness, the cologne he wore, and how warm he was.

"Step back," Noah ordered him.

Kieran stepped back, much to my surprise, and Noah instantly grabbed my hand and pulled me away.

"He's not going to hurt me," I whispered, but Noah wasn't looking at me.

"Stay away from her," Noah growled.

"You can't tell her what to do," Taylor said as he joined us.

"You three are nothing but trouble," Noah snapped. "You bring devastation wherever you go. Just let her live her life peacefully here."

"Like you're one to talk, Noah," Branson said. "You've caused your fair share of issues."

Noah's jaw clenched, the muscle flexing as he turned his head away. "You don't know what you're talking about."

"Cam," Sean called from the bookshelf he was looking at.

I looked between Noah and the Gods and took the quickest exit, hurrying over to Sean.

"What's up?" I asked him, standing so close, half my body touched his.

He noticed and put an arm around my waist before pointing at some books. "What do you think about these?"

I nodded and pointed out some others. "These would sell well, too, in our small town."

He smiled down at me. "I knew you would have a good eye for this type of thing. Thank you."

I returned his smile and resumed perusing the shelves. "Oh, this one!" I exclaimed and grabbed a book. I turned and was surprised to see the Gods gone.

"They said they'd catch up with you later," Tamara whispered from my side.

I looked at her and scowled. "Where'd your guy go?"

She smiled. "To get us some drinks and snacks."

"What about this one?" Sean asked and held out a book to me.

I read the book and rolled my eyes. "My mother would likely buy this religious drivel, so it should sell quickly in your store."

Sean nodded and added it to the stack he had under his arm.

"Here," I offered and held out my hands.

He considered me a moment and then set the books in my arms.

I followed him around and let him pick out more books, adding it to the stack that was growing heavier and heavier by the moment.

"You've got a lot of books here," I commented to one of the teenagers manning the booth, a willowy girl with straight brown hair.

She nodded. "Our grandma had lots in her storage."

"They're going to sell really well at my store," Sean whispered. "I feel like these will sell too fast."

I chuckled. "That's not a problem."

"Empty shelves are a problem," he muttered.

"I'll borrow a few of mine," I told him.

He looked at me, his eyes wide with horror. "You will not! Your books are your books, not to be sold at my store."

"You already asked to borrow them," I reminded him.

"Borrow, not sell," he said quickly.

I smiled and patted his arm. "I understand. Resume your browsing."

Tamara's boyfriend returned, and I waved at him, almost dropping the books in my arms and having to squat down to catch them.

"Let me help," Noah said and took half of the stack from me.

"You okay?" I asked him.

He exhaled. "Sorry for earlier. Kieran and I have never gotten along."

"He and I are just friends," I whispered. "Like you and I."

He cringed and nodded. "You don't need to explain yourself. I know the girls at the school consider them like gods. It's okay."

"They aren't gods," I said and rolled my eyes when he looked at me. "They're guys, just like you and Sean. Just normal guys."

"Seriously, you don't need to butter me up," he said.

"I'm not buttering anyone up," I said. "Just telling you how it is. I just came here a few weeks ago. I'm not in a relationship with anyone or set on anyone. I don't care that the girls here think they're gods. They're polite and so far have been nice to me. That's all I know. You've been nice to me, too, and so you're on an equal playing field."

"You are definitely not like the girls here," he whispered.

"I will take that as a compliment," I said with a laugh.

"It was intended that way," he said.

"Oh, look at this one!" Sean exclaimed and handed me another book. He looked at Noah. "Oh, hey. I didn't see you there."

Noah rolled his eyes. "I bet you didn't."

"This looks good," I said and added it to the stack in my arms, but Noah took it and added it to his instead.

"Okay, I think I'm done in this place," Sean said, looked at my arms and Noah's and chuckled. "Yeah, definitely done."

We headed to the teenagers running it, and Sean haggled prices with them. I was surprised when he haggled for a lower price from them before paying and heading off with a wide smile.

"That should be enough for the week," Noah said, took the books from me, and put them in a canvas bag he had on his arm.

"Where did you get the bag?" I asked.

"I bring it every time because Sean always forgets," he answered.

Sean chuckled. "Guilty, as charged."

"Want to look around and see what else we can find before we leave?" Noah asked me.

I nodded. "Sure."

As soon as I said it, I regretted it because we found ourselves at a booth with the guy who had caused us issues before.

Sean pushed me away from that one and to the next one, but I could see the guy following us a few people behind.

"You know him?" I asked Sean.

He nodded. "He's strange, even by our measure. I usually avoid him, but it seems that you have fascinated him."

"Not on purpose," I muttered.

"It's okay. He's from here, so he shouldn't cause you issues in our town."

That was good to hear. I didn't need to deal with another crazy in my life.

"Oh," I breathed as I looked at set of rings on display at a nearby table. "These are gorgeous."

"You have a good eye," the older man said. "These are real gemstones that I found on my property."

"Wow," I whispered and picked up an amethyst ring.

"Like purple?" he asked, glanced at my hair, and smirked.

I nodded. "I do." I looked at the price and sighed softly. It was way more than I could afford. "Your items are beautiful," I said. "Thank you for letting me view them."

He nodded and waved as we left.

"Cam!" Tamara called as she and her boyfriend caught up.

"Hey," I said and smiled at her.

"You guys about done?" she asked.

We all nodded.

She pouted and looked up at her boyfriend. "I guess I'm going to be leaving soon."

He stuck his bottom lip out in a pout, too. "So soon?"

"We can go get some food first and give you time to hang out," Sean said. "I know I'm hungry. What about you?"

Noah nodded. "Famished."

"Me, too!" I exclaimed.

Tamara beamed and mouthed, "Thank you," to us before letting the guy steer her away.

"Cam," Taylor said softly behind me.

I spun, surprised to find him alone. "Hey, Taylor. What's up?"

He looked at Sean and Noah. "Can I talk to you alone really quick?"

I nodded and hurried over to him. "What's up?"

"Are you okay?" he asked, his eyebrows pinched together.

Wow. It had been a long time since someone besides my mom legitimately worried about me.

I smiled and hugged him. "I'm good. Thank you."

He hugged me back and exhaled. "Good. I wanted to check before we left."

"Tell the others I will call you tonight, okay?" I requested.

He smiled and kissed my cheek. "We will wait for your call, milady."

I was blushing, I was certain of it, but it didn't matter to me. Watching Taylor leave and join up with Kieran and Branson just made me want to run after them.

"Totally not affected," Noah said with a scoff.

I looked at him with a scowl. "Really?"

He rubbed a hand down his face. "Sorry. Ignore me. I've had issues with them for a few years. I'm sorry to add you to our issues."

"Exclude me from any issues you have with them. I don't know any of you yet," I said. "I would like to get to know you better, but I'm not going to do it at the expense of my sanity or ability to relax."

"Sorry," he said again, looking genuinely apologetic.

"You are forgiven," I said with a smile.

Sean led the way to a truck that was selling tacos. We paid, got our tacos, and walked to an open grassy area to sit and eat them.

I devoured the delicious food, but quickly realized I didn't like it as much as some of the California food trucks I'd eaten from.

"You are disappointed?" Sean asked.

"A little," I admitted. "California has some really tasty food trucks."

"Maybe you could make some food for us," Wade suggested, joining us out of the blue.

I laughed and shook my head. "Not a chance. I suck at cooking. Mom keeps trying to make a proper woman out of me, but I can't cook anything correctly. It's not just baking."

"I would eat anything you gave me," the guy who I'd bumped into earlier said.

"Dude, beat it," Noah snapped.

"Call me," the guy said and dropped a piece of paper on the ground between all of us.

I swallowed nervously, not looking directly at him or the paper, my eyes focused on a space of grass that was currently unoccupied.

"Go on," Sean said. "Leave her alone."

The guy's legs moved out of my sight, and I exhaled loudly once I was certain he was gone. "Fuck." With a thump, I fell backwards onto my back on the grass and closed my eyes.

Did I just give off a vibe for these people to want to come after me? Was I just a freak that attracted other freaks?

"Cameron?" someone called.

I looked up, and locked eyes with one of the gang members I'd known in California.

I immediately got up, dropped my head, and ran from the area to the porta-potties.

A few minutes later, I stepped out to find Sean and Noah waiting for me.

"Let's give Tamara ten more minutes, and then we will head home," Sean said. "We can just walk among the stalls."

I didn't answer, my eyes on the ground.

Couldn't I just enjoy life like a normal teenager for a week? Not even one damn week.

"I'm sorry," I whispered.

"Why are you apologizing?" Sean asked.

"I shouldn't have come. All I ever do is cause people problems," I said. I rubbed my left wrist, the one with the most scars.

Sean reached over and took my right hand, stopping me. "You didn't do anything wrong. Stop. That guy is an anomaly and it wasn't your fault."

It was, though. I always brought them or attracted them. I was a magnet for trouble.

I turned, pulling away from Sean and looked at the ground. "Maybe it's better if I just wait by the car."

"I don't think—" Noah started, but Sean tossed me the keys.

"If you want to wait inside of the car, that's fine. I'll grab your books from the lady you purchased from earlier and load them for you," Sean said.

I smiled, though it was strained, and nodded. "Thanks."

As quickly as possible, I hurried through the crowd to the SUV, climbed inside, and locked all of the doors.

It wasn't likely that anyone would sneak into the vehicle here, but I didn't want to take any chances.

I had learned my lesson on that one.

I lay on my side on the seat, letting my eyes close as I tried to relax, but relaxation never came.

What felt like hours later, everyone returned, making me sit up and unlock the doors so they could load everything into the back of the SUV.

I handed the keys to Sean as he climbed into the driver's seat. "Here," I whispered.

"Here," he said back and held out the piece of paper the guy had dropped.

I took it despite wanting to just burn the stupid thing instantly.

"I don't want this," I whispered as Tamara climbed inside, looking sad.

Sean shrugged. "It wasn't my call to make."

"Thanks," I whispered.

CHAPTER NINE

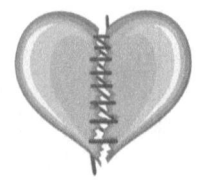

I tossed the paper into the trash as soon as I got home, deciding to let it rot there.

My phone rang almost immediately, making me shriek and my pulse race.

The caller ID showed Kieran.

"Hello?" I asked softly.

"Hey," Kieran said. "Can I come over?"

"Sure," I said. I had almost said, 'please', instead because I was so freaked out.

"Be there in five," he said and hung up.

I looked at my phone with a scowl.

It was still the early afternoon, so I had plenty of time to go outside and talk to a boy before my mom freaked out, but if he brought the other two with him, it would definitely spell trouble.

Mom did not like my ideas of being with multiple guys at once. I had brought it up once, and her cursing had made me certain never to bring it up again.

Instead of waiting for him to come, I snuck out of the

house while Mom was distracted by the television and sat on my porch.

"Cam," Kieran called from the tree that was nearest my window.

I stood from the porch and walked to him, not wanting him to see how much I needed to see him. Or see how much his presence after the encounter with that guy earlier made me feel safe.

"Hey," I said as I stopped before him and leaned against the tree.

"Hug?" he asked, standing stiffly beside the tree.

I shrugged and instantly, he enveloped me.

"I'll make sure he doesn't bother you," he whispered.

"Don't make promises you can't keep," I whispered back, pulling away from him.

He scowled at me. "What?"

I sighed. "Sometimes things happen to people that you can't control. Don't take it personally, okay?"

To my utter disbelief, he leaned down and brushed his lips across mine. "I will try my hardest to keep him away from you," he whispered afterwards.

My lips tingled even after the contact was done, and I stared up at him like a lost lamb.

"Why did you come here?" I finally managed to ask.

"You were really upset earlier. I could tell that guy sparked some fear in you and I wanted to make sure you knew that we would look out for you," he said.

I rolled my eyes. "You can't just stay at my house and watch in case someone might come looking for me."

He brushed some of my hair away from my face and said, "No, but I can make sure that you know you are safe. We will come help you whenever you call. No matter the time of day or night. If you need us, just call. Okay?"

It was more than I had been offered from any of my previous friends.

I nodded while biting my lip to keep from saying anything.

He rubbed his thumb across my lower lip, pulling it from between my teeth. "You should stop biting your lip so much. You're going to give yourself a sore."

"If I never date you, are you still going to stay my friends?" I asked him suddenly.

He considered me a moment before saying, "I'm not talking to you because I want to get in your pants, Cam. I'm talking to you in hopes of keeping my friend safe."

I leaned up on my tiptoes to kiss his lips and said, "Good answer," before turning and hurrying back into my house.

I wasn't surprised to see a goodnight text from him, but I was surprised by the texts from Noah and Sean. I responded saying goodnight to them as well and lay on my bed with a smile on my face.

Yes, scary things had happened, but the guys had taken care of it.

Maybe it wasn't such a bad thing to have so many guys attracted to me.

With so many people worried about me, I was much safer than I was before.

Maybe things wouldn't be so bad here.

Maybe.

The anxious tingling at the base of my skull told me otherwise.

It felt like someone was watching me.

Who? There was no way the guy we had seen earlier knew where I lived.

Right?

Right?

Somehow, I fell asleep and when I woke, I didn't sense the feeling of being watched.

I trudged to school feeling even more tired than I had left on Friday.

"You okay?" Sean asked as I walked by his store.

I stopped and looked at him. "Sorry. I was spacing out."

He hugged me and kissed the top of my head. "Have a good day at school, Cam."

I nodded and walked robotically to school. Now tired *and* shocked at the affection from Sean.

Tamara stood outside the grounds with her hands on her hips and her foot tapping. "Took you long enough."

"Sorry," I said and walked beside her to our first class.

"You okay, girl?" she asked softly.

I shrugged. "Yeah."

"Not sleep well?" she asked.

I shook my head.

"Want to talk about it?" Wade asked as he joined us.

"Morning, Cam," Noah greeted.

"Morning," I greeted him back.

"What? I don't get a morning?" Tamara asked, hands on her hips.

"Morning, Tamara," he said.

"No. It's too late now," Tamara said with a scoff.

"So, what's your prince's name?" I asked with a smirk.

She giggled. "Gorgeous, isn't he?"

I nodded. "Hot with like ten T's."

She giggled again.

"Cam!" Branson called out.

We were almost to our first period classroom, but I stopped and turned towards the direction his voice had come from.

Branson, Taylor, and Kieran walked towards me, all smiling.

"We're going to our class," Wade said and pulled Noah away.

Noah gave me a sad look, glared at the Gods, and then turned away, looking sad again.

"You look tired," Taylor said softly.

"That is not how a girl wants to be greeted," Tamara said and tsked her tongue. "I thought you Gods would have better manners?"

"Sorry," Taylor apologized.

"Trouble sleeping?" Kieran asked, stepping closer to me.

I nodded and dropped my eyes to my feet. "Yeah."

"You could have called," he whispered and tapped my bottom lip, which I hadn't even realized I had begun to chew on.

"Called? You gave her your phone number?" Sylvia asked.

We all turned to look at her.

She wore a beautiful green summer dress that made her look like she was auditioning for the part of a girl next door. Her hair was curled perfectly and bounced as she walked closer. Her hands went to her slim hips and she glared at me. "What part of leave them alone don't you—"

"Back down, Sylvia," Kieran spat, his words almost a growl. "You do not get to decide who can and cannot be friends with us. Last time I checked, you were just another person at this school, not my mother or anyone of consequence. So, back the hell off and leave Cameron alone."

"What?" she gaped, taking a step back like he had slapped her.

"Cameron is our friend. Don't interfere with that or you'll regret it," Taylor threatened her.

"Let's all calm down," I said, my hands shaking. "Sylvia, the guys and I are just friends and—"

"You're a slut, aren't you? You were on a date with that geek this weekend and now you're trying to sully the Gods. I heard girls in California were easy, but I didn't know they had no shame," she said.

I turned, fist clenched in preparation, but Tamara punched Sylvia before I could.

"Call my friend a slut one more time and see what happens," Tamara said softly.

Why was her soft voice more frightening than her loud one?

"You bitch!" Sylvia screamed and pressed her hand to her cheek. "You are going to get into so much trouble for that."

Tamara crossed her arms over her chest. "Bet me."

"What?" Sylvia asked, completely taken back.

"You go to the principal to tattle on Tamara for hitting you, and we go to him to explain how you threatened Cameron for just talking to us," Branson said. "Pretty sure we know who the principal likes better."

Tamara smirked. "The Gods rule, remember?"

I'd heard someone else say that phrase about the trio at my back. I had not expected it to be used to help me.

Sylvia huffed, looked at me with a glare that I was certain meant this wasn't over, and then flip her perfect hair over her shoulder before strutting away in her perfect dress and perfect body.

As soon as she was gone, the adrenaline left me and I felt lightheaded.

"Kieran? Catch me?" I whispered.

Strong arms wrapped around me before I even started to fall. "I got you, Lavender."

"Deep breaths," Tamara coaxed. "The evil witch is gone."

"What if...she comes back with flying monkeys?" I asked, taking the deep breaths and trying to joke to ease the tension and anxiety.

"I'll drop a house on her," Tamara said. "No problem."

The bell rang, and I forced myself to stand out of Kieran's arms and open my eyes. "I'm sorry," I said and smoothed my hair down.

Kieran pulled me into a hug and whispered into my ear, "Sit with us at lunch, please?"

"I, uh..."

"Please," he whispered again.

"Okay," I agreed.

He hugged me harder and then grabbed Taylor and started jogging across the campus towards their classroom.

Branson shoved my lower back and Tamara's to herd us into the classroom. "Sorry we're late," he called out to the teacher. "My fault."

"Don't let it happen again," Mrs. Adkins grumbled and then returned to taking roll.

We sat down, and I turned to him with an arched brow.

"Perks of being a god," he whispered back and waggled his eyebrows.

I covered my mouth to stop from laughing and shook my head.

These boys were ridiculous.

Things went as normal as any other school day, until lunch. Tamara had assured me that it was fine that I sat with the Gods occasionally.

We both weren't sure how Noah or Wade would take it, but since I wasn't in a committed relationship with anyone, it didn't really matter. I just had to make sure they knew my friendship with them didn't change.

Kieran waited at the cafeteria entrance for me, one leg bent as he leaned against the brick building.

Several girls surrounded him, chatting with bright smiles, gazing up at him like he was the sun.

Stopping in the middle of the walkway, I watched as he talked to them, his eyes bright, his smile warm, and the brooding male I knew was nowhere to be seen. Was this an act? Or was the Kieran I spent time with an act? Were they both acts? Did anyone know the real Kieran?

His gaze drifted over the heads of the girls and landed on me. He said something to the girls while still staring my direction, gently pushed them aside, and walked straight to me. People moved out of his way, which was a good thing because otherwise he would have run over a few.

Who was this guy?

"Cam?" he whispered. "Why are you looking at me like that?"

"How am I looking at you?" I asked.

"Like you're mad," he said. He reached up and tapped the spot between my eyebrows. "Your eyebrows are pinched together here." He looked down at my lips. "And your mouth is arched down in a frown."

"I'm not mad," I said, which was the truth. "Just wondering if you'll ever show me the real you or if you pretend with me like you do with them." I tilted my head towards the girls who still hadn't moved from the spot he'd left them.

He didn't look towards them. "I don't put on an act with you like I do them. I have to act a certain way with them because of my parents."

"Does that mean you'll treat me differently when you're around people you have to act a certain way with? Or that you'll ignore me if your parents are around?" I asked softly.

"Of course not," he said.

I shrugged. "I just need to know so it doesn't catch me off guard. Or, if I see you with your parents, so I know not to try to talk to you."

"You're being ridiculous again," Taylor said from behind me.

"I'm not. I've seen two-faced people a lot in my life. You'd be surprised how many gang members there are in school and fly under the radar there," I said.

"Come on, let's eat," Taylor said.

Kieran looked down at me with a scowl.

I walked around him, following Taylor to the table that was always open for them.

Standing before the empty table, I asked, "Where should I sit?" Since I didn't really pay that close attention to them the previous week, I did not know if they had certain seats they preferred.

"Wherever you want," Kieran said.

I sat in the seat that had the back to the wall, so I would be able to see if anyone approached us.

"Figured you would pick that one," Kieran said with a smirk.

"You getting food?" Taylor asked.

I pulled my sack lunch from my backpack. "Nope. I brought my own."

Kieran sat on my right and pulled his own sack lunch out. "Same."

"Branson is likely already in line," Taylor said. "I'll go find him and be back soon."

I nodded and pulled my sandwich out.

Kieran pulled out a sandwich, chips, and a soda. "Why couldn't you sleep last night?"

The bite of sandwich I had just taken got stuck in my

throat, and I coughed and tried to pull out my drink, but Kieran held out his soda, so I drank it quickly. "Thanks."

He took back the drink and just stared at me while he took a bite of his sandwich.

"I felt like someone was watching me," I admitted. "It made it hard to sleep."

He set his sandwich down. "Why didn't you call me?"

I glanced around and sure enough, lots of people were looking at us and whispering. Sylvia and her crew were trying really hard to prove they weren't paying any attention to us by turning the completely opposite way, which made me smirk.

"Cam?" he asked, getting my attention back on him.

"I'm not going to call you every time I have a strange feeling or get a little scared. If I did that, you might as well just move in," I said and shook my head.

"Did you see anyone?" he asked.

I shook my head. "I didn't look out the window, though."

"Could have been a raccoon," Branson said from across from me.

My head snapped up as I looked at him and Taylor. "When did you get here?"

"When you were staring at the table after finally stopping your coughing fit," Taylor answered.

Wow, I needed to get better about paying attention to my surroundings. I used to be really good about it, but since the move I had let my guard down way too many times.

"Friday night, will you hang out with us?" Taylor asked.

Snagging a chip from Kieran's bag, I chewed up before asking, "Doing what?"

"Watching the meteor shower," Branson said. "It's going to happen for two nights, but Friday night is going to be the best night for it."

I looked at the three jocks around me. "You like watching meteor showers?"

They scowled at me.

"What? You don't think we can like watching rocks burn up in the atmosphere?" Taylor asked.

"You guys would get laughed at by the football players of my last school," I said.

"We get laughed at by some of the players here, but we don't care. It's pretty," Branson said.

Kieran held out his bag of chips, and I frowned. He smirked. "Not as tasty if they're offered?"

"Exactly," I said with a nod.

Sometimes it was like he could read my mind.

"How come you guys were at the rummage sale?" I asked softly. I didn't want the eavesdroppers to hear this conversation. Maybe I should have waited until we weren't in such a public area.

"We go most weekends to help out my Nana," Branson said. "She always has a booth there to sell stuff."

Oh.

"You're cute and all, but not cute enough to go all stalker mode on," Taylor said with a wide smile.

Stalkers were something I hadn't dealt with, thankfully.

"Good to know I'm not cute enough for you," I said and stuck my lip out in a pout. "You're so mean, TayTay."

"TayTay?" he asked, his eyes wide. "No way. I do not like that nickname at all."

"So, who would you go stalker for?" I asked. I waited until Taylor took a drink before asking, "Sylvia?"

He gulped his drink down, turned, and coughed for a minute straight.

Branson and Kieran laughed at their friend while I smiled at his predictable reaction.

"Why are you guys single?" I asked.

"You haven't reached the appropriate friendship level to receive that information yet. Please ask again once you've reached level ten," Branson said with a wink.

"What level am I at now?" My sandwich was gone, but I was still hungry. I needed to remember to pack some carrots tomorrow.

"Hm..." Branson said and tapped his lips.

"Negative seven," Kieran answered.

I rolled my eyes. "I asked what level I am. Not what level Sylvia is."

All three laughed.

They had really nice laughs. The kind that made the room feel warm and bright. Like if I could make them laugh each day like this, everything would be fine.

"One second," Branson said, stood, walked to stand between Kieran and Taylor, and then bent and whispered too softly for me to hear over the loud cafeteria. They each looked at me several times while whispering.

Since Branson had abandoned his tray, I snagged a carrot from it, which earned me a frown, but he didn't say anything else.

Crunching happily on my carrot, I waited for them to finish their deliberation.

Branson sat down and then all three looked at me with serious faces.

"We have determined that you are at level three of our friendship," Kieran said.

"Three? Wow, that's higher than I thought. I figured I was a for sure one, maybe a two, but a three? Maybe you guys just make friends too easy."

"We could downgrade you if you want?" Kieran said with a shrug.

I pushed his shoulder and laughed. "Rude."

Lunch finished, and I wasn't too surprised when they each asked for a hug before we separated.

"How'd it go?" Tamara asked as she caught up to me outside the cafeteria.

I smiled. "Pretty well, actually. They continue to surprise me."

"Good," she said and linked our arms together. "Now, let's get to our favorite class, PE!"

I groaned, but followed her.

Sylvia glared at me as she walked by in the locker room.

At this point, there was really nothing I could do. She would hate me even if I was nice to her. So, I would just ignore her and hope she left me alone.

I knew better than to let her see my back. She was a wounded lioness and would love to pounce at me at her first chance.

For the foreseeable future, I would need to keep my eyes open and guard up whenever she was around.

Girls like her wouldn't do something when I was with my friends. She would wait for an opportunity to find me alone to pounce.

That was an opportunity I would deny her.

CHAPTER TEN

"What are you reading?" I asked Sean, leaning on the counter and setting my chin in my hands as I looked at him with a smirk.

He set his book down and smiled, leaning on the counter in the same pose as me. "A story about a girl who moves to a new school and learns everyone is a shapeshifter."

My eyes widened. "You read romances?"

He arched a brow. "Yeah?"

"Sorry, I just didn't expect that from you," I admitted and straightened.

"I love good stories and there are often amazing stories in romance books," he explained.

"So, what's on the agenda tonight?" I asked.

The others were waiting outside for him to finish his shift, but I'd opted to come inside and tease him for reading on the job.

"Are you free Friday night?" he asked as he clocked out.

"Um, I actually have plans. Why?"

He frowned and glanced down at his feet before looking back at me. "What about Saturday night?"

"I'm free Saturday night," I said.

He smiled and it lit up his entire face. "Want to watch the meteor shower with me?"

Oh!

"Sure!" I agreed quickly.

"Well, me and the rest of the group," he said with a chuckle. "Tamara has the best spot for setting up the telescope."

My excitement dropped at the mention of the others being there. "Oh, right. Yeah. Sounds fun. I've never watched one through a telescope before."

He slung his bag over his shoulders and looked down at me. "What's wrong?"

I forced a smile and shook my head. "Nothing."

The scowl on his face seemed to say he didn't believe me, but he just opened the door for me, and we joined our already laughing group and walked down the street to Tamara's house.

We had to stop to wait for a truck to drive by at the corner where the café was and when I looked across the street at the post office, I saw someone in a dark jacket and sunglasses staring at me.

"Come on," Tamara said and tugged on my arm, pulling my gaze away from the guy.

I looked back, but he was gone.

We crossed the street and Noah stepped up to my side. "What's wrong?"

Paranoia was not my friend.

Knock it off, Cameron.

"Nothing," I said with a smile.

Of course there were people staring at you. You have purple hair.

People were the same everywhere, if someone looked different, they would stare.

The group talked about the meteor shower non-stop on the way to Tamara's place.

We finally got to her house and sat in our usual seats, but I was the only one who pulled out a book this night.

"Are you coming Friday?" Tamara asked.

I kept my nose in my book. "No. I'm coming Saturday."

"But Friday is the best night," Wade said.

"Sorry, I have plans," I said.

"Plans with them?" Noah asked.

"Hm?" I asked, pretending to be distracted by my book instead of answering him right away.

"The three stooges," he said.

I set my book down and turned to face him. "Why do you hate them?"

"Why are you defending them?"

I scowled. "I'm not defending anyone. I just asked you why you hate them."

"I don't hate them," he said. "I just can't stand how they think they're better than everyone. I can't stand that girls drool all over them." He stood, snatching his bag from the ground. "And I had hoped you were better than the girls here, but you've fallen into their trap, too."

"Trap? What trap is that? Of being my friend?" I asked.

"Friend? You call them kissing you friends?" he snapped.

I stood, my hands fisted, but shaking. "One, you are not my father or someone who can tell me what to do or how to act. I get enough of that from my religious mother. Two, I am not in a relationship with anyone, so me hanging out with guys, one, two, or a dozen, doesn't matter. Three, how do you know any of them kissed me?"

His mouth had opened to respond back to my statements, but at my question, his mouth snapped shut, his jaw clenched, and he turned away. "I'll see you guys tomorrow."

"Were you spying on me?" I called after him.

"No," he said and stopped. "I was outside trimming the stupid apricot tree and saw you two."

"Why are you so mad? I never told you we were exclusive and I've told them we're just friends. So, what right do you have to get so mad at me for making friends? Do you have any freaking idea how hard it is for me to make friends? I thought you all were a godsend, but now I think you might be my reminder of why I stopped making friends. I don't like being accused of things I didn't do. I don't like being made to feel like a bad person when I've done nothing wrong." Tears fell down my face in fat drops, splattering to the wooden porch at my feet.

Sean reached out towards me and I jumped back, yelping in fear.

Everyone stared at me with wide eyes.

Covering my face with my hands, I turned and ran across the yard and into my house, ignoring their shouts. I ran up to my bedroom, slammed my door closed, sat in the corner of my room with my knees to my chest, and tried to slow my sobbing breaths.

Someone knocked on the front door, and I heard Mom answer, but then the door closed and she came up the stairs.

"Cameron?" she called softly.

"N-no," I whispered.

"Okay, honey," she whispered back, walked down the stairs, and said something I couldn't hear before shutting the front door and locking it.

I dropped my head to my knees and cried.

Why did I always screw things up? Why couldn't I just be normal for once in my life and have friends like everyone else did?

My cell phone rang, text notifications went off one after the other, but I ignored them all.

Mom returned, and I heard her set something outside the door. "Dinner," she whispered.

Food sounded awful, especially with my mouth tasting like sawdust.

I had ruined something again.

At some point I dozed off, only to be woken by something hitting my window.

I crawled over, peeked out where I wouldn't be seen, and my eyes widened to find all three of the Gods standing beneath the tree by my window.

After wiping my face as best as I could, I opened the window.

"You weren't answering your phone," Kieran said.

"We got worried," Taylor added.

"Why are your eyes puffy?" Branson asked.

I rubbed at my face. "Sorry. I got in a fight with a..." Was it right to call him a friend? "I got in an argument and had a panic attack. I didn't want to talk to them so I ignored my phone."

"Can you come down?" Taylor asked.

I tilted my head as I listened for my mom, but the only sound was the television in her room, which meant she had likely fallen asleep with it on like usual.

"For a couple of minutes," I said.

Slowly, I opened my door so it wouldn't squeak and then quickly and quietly made my way down the stairs, outside, and around the house to them.

"What's up?" I asked.

All three hugged me at once.

Against my wishes, the tears came again, and I clutched the shirt of the guy in front of me as I cried again.

"Who do we need to beat up?" Kieran asked.

"Me," Noah said.

I tensed, gripping the shirt in my hands even tighter.

The guy behind me and the one on my left moved to stand beside me.

"You?" Taylor asked.

I looked up and found I had grabbed onto Branson. He wiped my eyes with his thumbs and brushed my hair back from my face.

"Yeah. I acted like an idiot and upset her," Noah said. "I'm sorry, Cam. I shouldn't have said any of that or acted that way. You didn't deserve that."

"No, I didn't," I whispered.

"What did you say to her?" Kieran asked, his voice stern.

"Why are you three interested in her? Aside from her being pretty. Are you just looking to add her to your conquests? To be able to say she's yet another girl that would do anything for you?" Noah asked.

Kieran scoffed. "You know that's not us."

"Do I? All the girls at school would do anything for you. You could tell them to shave their heads bald and they would, even Sylvia," Noah said bitterly.

"You've always been jealous of us," Branson said, still looking down at me. "We don't care if you hate us, but don't take it out on Cam."

"You didn't answer my question," Noah said.

"We're friends," Taylor said.

"If things progress from there, we'll take it one day at a time," Kieran said and I saw his shoulders rise in a shrug.

"You mean more than you kissing her?" Noah asked.

"Ah, it makes sense now," Kieran said. "You took her on a date and thought you were going to beat us to her, but then saw me kiss her and got jealous. Well, Cameron and I are currently just friends. Just like you and she are."

Noah sighed. "I know. I know. I'm sorry. This isn't like me."

Part of me didn't believe him. Maybe this really was him. Maybe I was seeing the true Noah. I'd known a few couples where the guy was super jealous and possessive, but only showed it to her in private. Outside, to everyone else, they looked like a perfect couple. But if a guy even talked to her, he got pissed and yelled at her.

"Cam?" Noah called softly. "I'm sorry."

"Okay," I replied.

"Can I see you so I can apologize to your face?" he asked.

I turned my head, looking in the opposite direction and shook it against Branson's chest.

"She needs some time," Branson said.

At the edge of my house was an abnormal dark shadow. It looked like a...man.

"Branson, there's someone...!" I screamed and looked up at him.

Taylor and Kieran turned to face me, too.

I looked back at the spot, but there was nothing there.

"What?" Branson asked. "Did you see something?"

"I thought...I thought I had," I whispered. Was I going crazy?

"We'll check it out. Branson stay with her," Kieran said.

Watching them leave made my heart race. What if there really was someone there?

Kieran walked to a truck parked on the street, reached in the back, and pulled out a gun.

I gaped at him. "You have a gun?"

"It's a hunting rifle," Branson said. "We all have them."

Okay, this was not what I had expected.

Kieran and Taylor walked around the side of my house, and

I was even more scared now. I didn't want anyone getting shot because of me.

They came around the opposite side, having made a circle and Kieran put his gun away.

"We didn't see anyone," Taylor said.

I rubbed my face. "It was probably just the stress making me see things. Sorry."

"Don't apologize. Just the other night, Taylor raced outside because he thought someone was trying to steal stuff and it was just a family of raccoons going through his trash," Branson said, smiling down at me.

"Big ass raccoons," Taylor grumbled.

"Technically, they were trying to steal stuff, it was just garbage," I said.

Taylor draped his arm around my shoulders and pulled me against his side. "See? She gets it!"

I leaned my head into Taylor and then grimaced. "You smell!"

Taylor raised his arm up and sniffed his armpit. "Whoa! I totally do. My bad."

"Stop putting your stench on her," Kieran said and pulled me closer to him, away from Taylor.

"Were you guys working out or something?" I asked.

"Yeah. We work out to help with our stress and frustrations. When you didn't answer we thought maybe you were mad at us for making you eat lunch at our table or something bad had happened," Kieran said.

Something bad had happened, but just emotionally.

"You really are different with her," Noah said softly.

It wasn't until he spoke that I remembered he was there. The Gods were so large that they had blocked my sight of him.

"Why are you still here?" Kieran asked. "She said she

doesn't want to see you tonight. Leave her alone and try again tomorrow."

"I'm sorry, guys," Noah said. "I shouldn't let an old grudge still have this much sway over me."

"No, you shouldn't," Branson said.

"Alright, I'm going. I'm sorry, Cam."

Saying anything to him right now was out of the question.

His footsteps crunched on the road as he walked away.

After a moment, all three of the Gods faced me again.

"You okay?" Taylor asked.

I wrapped my arms around myself and nodded. "I appreciate you coming and checking on the house."

"I told you we would come if you called. You should have just called after it happened," Kieran said.

I rolled my eyes. "It would have made it so much better if I ran from Tamara's house to mine and then you showed up two minutes later."

Kieran smirked. "I could have confronted him in front of his friends and shown them all that we know you aren't like the other girls at school."

Wasn't I? It had only been a week of talking to them, and I was already more comfortable with them than I had been with any of my other friends.

Honestly, I always got along better with guys anyway. They tended to say what was actually on their minds, beat the crap out of each other, and then forgive and move on.

Girls weren't like that. We held grudges for years. Mom said there was a lady from high school that had been jealous of her and Dad and she saw the lady ten years after high school and the lady still treated her poorly just because Dad had chosen her.

If Dad were here, things might have been different. He

wouldn't have let us live in that crappy area of California, and I wouldn't have gone to that awful school.

I didn't blame Mom. No, it was all my own decisions and actions that were the problem. It just would have made it easier to avoid those types of situations if we had lived in a nicer area.

"You aren't like the other girls at school," Taylor said softly, putting his finger beneath my chin to make me look up at him.

I stared into his eyes and smirked. "I know. I'm worse."

Kieran sighed and shook his head. "Self-deprecating."

"How come he got a kiss?" Branson asked and pouted.

"Because I'm the best-looking," Kieran said. "Obviously."

"Please, we all know that's me," Taylor said.

"I'm the nicest," Branson said.

"I'm just lucky, I guess," Kieran said and shrugged. "Maybe you just need to be nicer to her."

"Cam?" Tamara called out softly.

"Here," I called back.

Tamara walked across the grass to us, her eyes widening when she saw the Gods. "Oh, I didn't know you had company. I heard voices and got worried." She looked at me. "You okay?"

I shrugged. "No, but I should get over it soon."

"You mean shove it down into a bottle with the rest of your emotions and not face them?" Kieran asked and folded his arms across his chest.

"What's up with these boys? Why aren't they like the stupid jocks that television shows?" I asked Tamara. "They keep saying smart things and it's throwing me for a loop."

Tamara grabbed me suddenly and hugged me. "He was just jealous and didn't mean what he said. You aren't a bad person and the rest of us gave him a real good scolding after you left. Even Mama came out and smacked him on the back of the head."

I hugged her back and laughed. "I wish I had seen that."

"Mama was pissed. Told him his stupid head and cruel words were the reason he was single and he shouldn't blame a girl for being a girl."

"I like your Mama," Branson said.

Tamara pushed back from me and glared at him. "You stay away from my Mama. If you boys start coming around, she's going to want you over more and that's out of the question."

"You don't like us?" Taylor asked with a pout. "But we're always nice to you, Tammy."

Tamara turned and glared at him. "Do not call me that. You know I hate that name."

"Oh, I see! He likes adding that sound to the end of names," I said. Everyone turned and looked at me like I had lost my mind. "He called me Cammy the other day."

Taylor shrugged. "It fit."

"Cammy does fit you," Tamara said with a smirk.

I smacked her arm playfully. "Don't encourage them!"

"You boys better not hurt her or I'll make you pay," Tamara told them. "And don't you dare make her choose between our friends and you. Noah will straighten out and things will return to normal. Besides, she isn't committed to any of you."

"We know and we wouldn't make her choose," Kieran said seriously.

"Oh, Sean told me to tell you to stop by the store before school," Tamara said. She leaned closer and whispered, "He was furious with Noah for talking to you like he did. I thought he was going to punch him."

My mouth dropped open. "Sean? Sean wouldn't hurt a fly."

She nodded. "I know. That's why I was so shocked. Anyway, I got to head back inside. You boys act right. God's watching!"

Kieran rolled his eyes. Taylor and Branson waved to her.

For the first time, I had a female friend that actually felt like a friend. Not an ally or someone who would have my back in a fight. An actual friend who cared about my feelings as well as my health.

"You look confused," Taylor said.

"I've just never had a friend like her," I explained.

"She's one of a kind, for sure. It was awesome to watch her punch Syliva. That wench has been rude to Tamara since she came here and we all know why," he said.

"Because she's prettier than Sylvia?" I asked.

They nodded.

Branson looked over at Tamara's house. "And just because she's black. Sylvia's family is one of the oldest in this town and their beliefs and morals are that old as well. That wasn't the first time Tamara has punched her. That was the day we decided never to date Sylvia or have anything to do with her. We don't associate with racists or bigots."

"She acts like you're dating though?" I said, confused. "Like, she put her arm through yours and asked about hanging out on the weekend."

"She always does that. Doesn't matter how many times we tell her to stop," Kieran growled. "She's annoying."

"Super annoying," Taylor said.

"We've told her several times that we aren't interested in her and will never date her and she doesn't care. She won't give up. We have to be a little nice because our parents go to church with theirs, but I'd love to tell her off," Kieran said.

"You sort of told her off and threatened her about me today," I whispered and looked down at my feet.

"We'd do it again in a heartbeat," Branson said and hugged me.

"This is not level three behavior," I told them, my voice muffled as my face was pressed into Branson's shirt.

"You've been upgraded to level four," Kieran said.

"Does that mean I get a trophy or something for reaching the next level?" I asked and looked up at Branson with a smile.

He bent and kissed me, just his lips ghosting across mine.

I blinked, shocked.

"Hey! No fair, that was what I was going to do," Taylor huffed behind me.

"Isn't that more of a prize for you than me?" I asked, trying to hide how it had affected me.

"That's true," Kieran said. "Now you owe her double."

"I'll think of something," Branson said and stepped back from me. He looked back at my house and said, "We should do another sweep before we leave."

"Agreed," Kieran said. "Taylor, stay with her this time."

Taylor stepped up to my side and draped his arm across my shoulders. "Understood, Captain."

Kieran rolled his eyes and then he and Branson walked off into the dark around my house.

"It'll be okay," Taylor said softly to me. "We look out for each other in this town and we'll make sure you're as safe as possible."

"Thanks," I whispered and shivered at just the thought that there could have been someone there.

Taylor pulled me closer and rubbed my arms, thinking I was cold.

Cold was the least of my fears.

CHAPTER ELEVEN

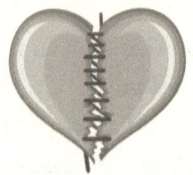

The guys had stayed for another twenty minutes or so before reluctantly agreeing to leave just so they could get some sleep.

Since I had run late, I hadn't had a chance to stop by the store to talk to Sean, but I had popped my head in and promised to see him after school.

I sat with the Gods at lunch again, but this time because I wanted to.

Noah didn't try to talk to me, but whenever I glanced in his direction, he was looking at me with pitiful eyes.

Saying things you didn't mean in the heat of the moment was something I was very familiar with, so I had already forgiven him. I just didn't want to go up to him and talk about it yet.

School ended and I felt myself starting to smile again after having a good day.

That smile was gone when I stepped out of the campus grounds and saw the guy from the rummage sale leaning against a car parked nearby.

He straightened when he saw me and smiled. "Hey! I finally found you."

Glancing around, I was dismayed to find none of my friends nearby.

Pulling my phone out, I dialed Kieran's number and just left it on, then put it in my pocket.

"What are you doing here?" I asked.

"I came to see you, of course," he said and stopped a little bit away from me.

Too close. He was too close, so I took a step back.

"Um, well, I'm just leaving the front of the school and have someone to meet," I said, giving Kieran directions on where to find me if he was listening like I hoped he was.

I tried to walk around the guy, but he stepped in front of me.

"Want to grab a bite to eat?" he asked.

"Sorry, I don't have time—"

"Come on," he said and reached out towards me. "I'll pay."

I stumbled back from him, my heart racing. "S-stop."

He frowned at me. "What's wrong? I just want to take you out for some food. I promise I'm really nice."

"Cameron!" Branson called as he ran over to me. "There you are! I was looking all over for you."

"Who is this?" the guy asked.

"I'm a friend," Branson said. "Who are you?"

"Someone who's leaving," Kieran said from the other side of the guy.

He turned around to face Kieran. "This is none of your business. I'm not doing anything wrong. I'm just talking to her. She's fine with it. We were just going to get a bite to eat together."

"No, we weren't," I said. "I told you I'm meeting someone."

He faced me and frowned. "Well, then tomorrow! I'll come tomorrow and we can get some food together."

"N-no," I stammered.

"She's not interested," Kieran said. "Leave her alone."

"Come on," Taylor said, grabbed my hand in his, and pulled me down the street.

"Hey! Wait!" the guy called out to me.

I ignored him, gripping Taylor's hand tightly as we walked away from the school.

"Taylor!" Sylvia called. "There you are. Wait, are you holding her hand?"

"I need to stop at the store to see Sean," I whispered, my breathing coming in pants.

"I thought you weren't dating anyone," Sylvia said. "And that she was dating that nerd."

"Not now, Sylvia," Taylor said.

"I'm not in a relationship with anyone," I told her. "Tay...I think I might faint."

"Almost to the store," Taylor said, slipped his arm around my waist, and increased our speed.

I heard the door open, cold air hit me, and Sean said, "Welcome...Cam? What happened?"

My vision swam, black dots covering most of my sight, but I saw Sean as I was placed on my back.

"Why is the princess fainting this time? Someone said something mean again?" Sylvia asked with a scoff.

"Why are you here?" Sean asked. "If you aren't buying anything get out."

"Don't talk to me like that Sean Sampson!" Sylvia snapped. "I could get you fired and—"

"Get out!" Taylor yelled. "Leave Cameron alone. I get that you're threatened by her, but just leave her alone."

"Don't yell at me!" she shouted.

"Then listen and go away!" Taylor shouted back.

"Cameron, can you hear me?" Sean asked and set his hand on my head.

"Th-the guy. He found me," I whispered.

"We're a pretty small county," Taylor whispered. "It wouldn't have been that hard for him to ask around about a girl with purple hair."

"Where are Branson and Kieran?" I asked and closed my eyes. If they got hurt by that guy because of me I wouldn't forgive myself.

"Probably trying to get that guy to leave and stop following you," Taylor said.

"What guy?" Sylvia asked. "Are you talking about Arthur? He asked me about Cameron yesterday and said you guys were friends?"

"This is your fault?" Taylor shouted. "You told him where she was?"

"He said they were friends, but he had lost her phone number," she said softly.

"You know Arthur is a freak," Taylor snapped.

"So is she!" Sylvia shouted back. "I figured they had to be friends."

"It's fine," Sean said. "We'll handle it."

"We're already taking care of it," Taylor said.

"Doesn't hurt to have backup," Sean said.

My vision finally started clearing, and my breathing evened out. "I'm sorry," I said and tears spilled down my cheeks. "I'm sorry."

"Cammy, don't apologize," Taylor said and squatted down to wipe some of the tears off my face, but they kept coming.

"I al-always attract problems and danger," I said, sat up, and got to my feet. I stumbled a second, and Sean grabbed my shoulders.

"You haven't done anything wrong," Sean said softly, calmly. He pulled me into his chest and hugged me. "It's okay."

"What a baby," Sylvia scoffed. "Some guy wants to take you out and you're acting like he tried to hurt you."

"Why are you still here?" Taylor shouted.

We heard the door of the store open and everyone turned.

"He's gone," Kieran said as he and Branson came inside.

"Kieran!" Sylvia said with excitement.

"She told him where to find Cam," Taylor told Kieran, glaring at Sylvia.

"What?" Kieran asked, his voice deadly quiet as he said that one word.

"I th-thought they were friends. He said they were friends," she said softly, her bravado gone.

"Get out," Kieran told her. "And don't come near us again."

"Wh-what?" she stammered, her eyes wide.

"You heard me," he said. He was practically vibrating with anger. "I don't want to see you or talk to you again."

"Kieran, we've been friends since kindergarten," she said and laughed, though it sounded forced.

"Is...is he going to come back?" I asked.

Kieran turned away from Sylvia and walked to me. "Most likely. We'll try to keep him away, though."

That was impossible. They couldn't keep someone away from me all the time.

Sean let me go and walked over, whispering to Branson who nodded his head every so often.

Kieran opened his arms, and I immediately stepped into them, letting him hug me.

"I'm sorry," I whispered.

"Stop apologizing for something that isn't your fault," he chastised me gently.

"Maybe I should change my hair, so I don't stand out so much." Honestly, I loved my hair and didn't want to change it, but I would if it would help me stay safe.

He leaned back and gently ran his fingers through my hair. "But I like this color. It suits you."

"I don't want someone getting hurt because of me," I told him, my eyes brimming with tears.

"What is going on? She's just some random new girl. Why are you treating her like she's a friend you've known your whole life?" Sylvia asked.

"Why is she still here?" Kieran asked.

"You've done enough for today," Sean. The door opened and he said, "Now, get out."

"Slut," she said before the door closed.

Maybe I was. Even though I wasn't sleeping with them, maybe I was a slut. An emotional one. Was that a thing? If it was, that's what I was.

"Ignore her," Kieran said.

"Easier said than done," Sean said with a bitter laugh.

"C-can you walk me home?" I asked.

"Not going to Tamara's tonight?" Sean asked.

I stepped away from Kieran to face him. "No. I don't really feel like hanging out right now."

"Because of Noah?" he guessed.

I nodded and rubbed my left arm. "A lot has happened the past couple of days."

"Which is why hanging out with friends is even more important," Taylor said. "So you aren't dwelling on the negative thoughts in your own mind all alone."

"He's right," Sean said. "If you don't want to see Noah, I'm sure Kieran would let you come over and hang out with them."

"You...you don't care that I'm hanging out with them?" I asked him.

Sean smiled. "Why would I care that you have friends? Noah and these three have issues that preceded you coming. We've never had issues."

"If he was a year younger, he probably would have been God number four," Kieran said and smiled at Sean.

Sean laughed and shook his head. "Please, we all know my looks are no match for you three. Plus, I suck at sports."

"True, you were terrible at football," Kieran teased.

Sean was wrong, though. He was just as attractive as the Gods. He totally could have been their fourth.

"What do you say, Lavender? Want to come hang out with us?" Branson asked.

I chewed on my lower lip. "I don't think my mom would be okay with me going over to a guy's house."

"Hm..." Taylor said and tapped his lips as he thought. "What if we came over to your house for a study session?"

I blinked. "What?"

"We have a test tomorrow in math. We could all come over and have a study session at your house, in your living room so your mom could keep an eye on us, and it would give us a chance for her to meet us and get to know us," he said. "Or we could have it on your lawn or something, but still where she could see us."

Mom did like hosting people.

"Let me call her and ask," I said. The most private place was the backroom with the books, so I called from there while browsing the shelves. "Hey, Mom, would it be okay if some friends came over for a study session? We'd just stay in the living room while we studied. Or, if you don't want them inside, I could—"

"Boys?" she guessed.

"Yeah," I said softly, flinching.

She sighed and then laughed softly. "Sure, but you have to stay where I can see you the entire time they are over. Understand? Not a single person goes up the stairs."

"Thanks, Mama," I whispered and almost cried.

"I'll start making snacks now," she said and hung up.

I walked out to find all four whispering together quietly by the window, looking outside with scowls.

"She said you could come over to study," I informed them.

"Perfect," Sean said. "I'll close up, and we can all walk that way together."

I walked up to him, hugged him around the waist, and rested my head on his chest. "Thank you for being understanding."

He hugged me back and placed a kiss on top of my head. "I'm just being a decent human. You don't need to thank me, but you're welcome."

"I'll come by tomorrow morning, okay?" I said.

He stepped back and nodded. "You better."

Once he had closed up, the five of us walked down the street towards Tamara's and my houses.

The looks we received were comical from the other teenagers.

We paused at Tamara's to say bye to Sean, who gave me another hug, and then waved to us as we continued to my house.

I opened the front door and called inside, "Mama, we're here."

The guys took their shoes off at the door before coming inside.

Mama walked out of the kitchen, wiping her hands on her apron, a wide smile on her face as she turned on host mode. "Welcome home." She froze a millisecond when she saw the guys. "Well, if it isn't the Gods of Sheldon High. I didn't know you were friends with the local celebrities, Cameron." She gave me a look that said I should have told her who was coming over.

"Please, just call us son," Kieran said, turning on his charm all the way up to eleven.

Mom's cheeks reddened slightly.

I rolled my eyes. Wonderful, even Mama was affected by them.

"Make yourselves comfortable. I'll have snacks and drinks ready soon," she said and giggled.

Dear Lord, she actually giggled!

"You're too kind," Branson said. "We'd have been fine with stale crackers and water."

Mama gasped. "You keep talking like that and I'll make you a full meal."

"Come on, guys. We need to study, remember?" I said, pulled out my math book, and set it on the coffee table.

Kieran sat on the left side of the couch, Taylor sat on the right side, and Branson sat on the floor across the table from us.

"Cameron, can you come here, honey?" Mama called.

I sighed softly. "Be right back," I whispered to them.

As soon as I got into the kitchen, she pulled me around the wall and hissed, "Why didn't you tell me it was them?"

"Mama, they're just boys. I didn't know you cared which boys they were."

"They are the most popular boys in the entire county! They're the star players and every mom wants their girl to date one of them. Are you dating them? They're gorgeous and you would make beautiful children with one of them."

I gaped at her. "You have gone insane! The south has rubbed its charm all over your thinking and turned you into one of them."

She tsked her tongue at me. "Don't talk so negatively." She peered around the wall at them before looking back at me and brushed some of my hair down in the back. "You're not sleeping with them, right? All joking aside."

"No, I'm not, Mama. We are just friends," I said.

She nodded. "Good." She looked back around the wall and then smiled at me. "If you did want to date one of them, though, I wouldn't be opposed to it."

I sighed and shook my head. "You are incorrigible. I'm going back out there."

She handed me a tray of sodas and glasses with ice in them. "Take this."

I took it dutifully and returned to the guys.

They each took a drink from the tray, and Kieran leaned over to whisper, "We would make some beautiful babies."

I gasped and smacked his arm. "Eavesdropping jerk!"

The three chuckled.

"Good to know we've got her permission," Taylor said and winked at me.

I covered my face with my hands and groaned, certain I was blushing.

"Hopefully, this means we can come over without trouble," Branson said.

"You should butter her up," Taylor suggested.

I let my hands drop to look at them.

Branson stood with a wicked smile. "That's a good idea." He turned and headed towards the kitchen. "Ma'am, do you need any help? I can carry any heavy items or grab things from high shelves if you need me to."

He disappeared into the kitchen, and I heard Mama giggle again.

I leaned back and closed my eyes as I let my head drop to the back of the couch. These guys were something else.

"Hey," Taylor said and poked my cheek. "We've got to study."

"Right. Right," I said and sat up.

Normally, my study sessions were full of everything except studying. This time, I spent the entire time studying. It was a bit surreal.

Branson brought out a tray of small sandwiches and immediately shoved two in his mouth.

"Manners," Kieran chastised him.

Two hours later, I stood and stretched. "Oh, I've been sitting too long."

"Dinner will be ready in an hour," Mama called out from the kitchen, then poked her head out. "You boys are staying, right?"

"We wouldn't miss it, ma'am," Kieran said and beamed.

She returned his smile and disappeared back into the kitchen.

"When is your first sports season?" I asked, obviously clueless about it.

"We actually started conditioning already," Taylor said. "We'll have to start attending practices next week. First game is in three weeks."

"Oh," I whispered sadly. Once they started attending practices and doing games, I wouldn't be able to spend much time with them. They'd be spending it all on the field.

"You're welcome to watch our practices," Branson said.

"I'll be going back to hanging out with Tamara after school," I said.

"Will you come to our games?" Kieran asked.

"Please!" Branson begged.

"You bet your butts she will be attending your games!" Mama said as she came out with refills. "Friends support each other."

Sighing in front of them would get me in trouble with her, so I just clamped my lips together.

"Awesome!" Branson cheered. "I can't wait."

"You boys think you'll go State again?" Mama asked.

My mouth dropped. Since when did she know anything about sports?

"We hope so," Taylor said and beamed. "We did last year and I'm sure we will get that trophy yet again."

"You guys are champions?" I asked, not sure what to actually call them.

Mama sighed. "Forgive my daughter, she's not much of a sports fan."

I shrugged. "Sportsball events are really my thing."

"Sportsball? Did you just call it sportsball?" Kieran asked with a smirk.

"It's a sport with a ball. Sportsball." I took a chug of my drink to avoid smiling back.

"Why don't you guys go outside for a little bit before dinner is done?" Mama suggested.

"Good idea," I said. "I need some fresh air and to stretch."

"Maybe we should start taking Cammy on our workouts," Taylor suggested.

Before I could say, "hell no," Mama gasped.

"That sounds like a great idea! She needs to get stronger and build up her endurance," she said.

Glaring at her was all I could do.

"We can definitely help with that," Branson said with a nod. "We'll do runs and weight lifting. We can start out light on the weights so she doesn't hurt herself and of course we would spot her."

"You aren't going to have time for that when your season picks up," I said, looking for a loophole out.

"We work out every single day," Kieran said with a smirk. "Would it be alright if Cam came over to my place on the weekends to workout with us?"

Oh, these boys were so good and devious. They were setting it up so I could come over to their place and my mom was eating it up.

"Of course!" Mom exclaimed. "I'm so glad you've made some good friends, Cameron. Thank you, boys, for giving my girl a chance." She glared at my hair. "Even with her odd hair."

"We love her hair," Kieran said and tugged on a strand as he stood beside me. "It's unique, just like her."

Mama smiled and then shooed us toward the door. "Outside. Go get some fresh air while I finish up dinner."

"You sure you don't need help?" Branson asked.

"Out you four," she ordered.

We walked outside and stopped on the porch at the sight of Arthur talking to Sean in front of Tamara's house.

Too late to realize what was going on, Arthur turned and spotted us. He smiled wide and started to walk towards the house, but Sean grabbed his arm.

"Oh, shit," I whispered.

"Cam!" Tamara called and ran over.

"Stay here," Kieran ordered. "Taylor, stay with her."

Branson and Kieran headed towards Arthur and Sean who were shouting at each other now.

"Cameron, what's going on? Isn't that the guy from the rummage sale?" Tamara asked.

"He found me at the school," I said. "He doesn't know how to take no for an answer."

"I've heard he stalked some other girls," Tamara whispered. "I thought that was just rumors, though."

Kieran and Branson started talking to Arthur, too.

He tried to walk around them towards my house, but Kieran pushed him on the chest, making him stay back.

Arthur punched Kieran on the jaw and Branson punched Arthur. And then Sean came over.

"No. No. No," panted.

"What's all the shouting?" Mama asked as she came out. She saw the boys fighting, went back inside, and then returned with a bat in her hand.

"Mama," I gasped.

"Ma'am, we've got it," Taylor said.

"Like hell you do," Mama snapped. "I'm not letting someone hurt my girl again. I'll go to jail before I go through that again." She looked at Tamara, "You go tell your Daddy to get his ass outside and scare that boy off before I beat some sense into him."

Tamara nodded. "Yes, Ma'am," and ran into her house.

A few seconds later her dad came out, sized up the situation, shoved Arthur away from the others and yelled at him while pointing away from the house.

Sean had blood dripping from his nose. Kieran's cheek was red. Branson's knuckles were bloody.

"Not again," I whispered.

"Who is that?" Mama asked.

"Stalker," I whispered.

Taylor gripped my hand and said, "It'll be okay, Cammy."

"What happened?" Mama asked. "How did you get involved with that guy?"

"It wasn't her fault," Taylor said. "We were at the rummage sale in the town over, and he started talking to her and wouldn't leave her alone. He tracked her here and cornered her after school. We got her away from him, but he doesn't take no for an answer easily."

Mama sighed and shook her head.

"I didn't mean for it to happen," I whispered. "I didn't talk to him or give him my name or number or anything. I'm sorry."

"Baby, this isn't your fault. Danger and creeps just seem to be drawn to you," Mama said. She eyed Taylor. "You better not be a creep, too. God or not, I'll take you out if you hurt my girl."

Taylor smiled. "I swear I'm not a creep and I would never hurt Cameron."

Arthur had left, but Tamara's dad, Sean, Branson, and Kieran were still talking.

"I'm going to go see what's up," Taylor said. "Stay with your mom."

"We can't move again," Mama whispered.

"I know. I don't want to move again," I said. "I'm sorry."

"Stop apologizing, Cameron," she ordered me and set her bat on the ground. She grabbed my left wrist, which I hadn't realized I was gripping. "Promise me you won't do that again?"

I looked down at her hand on my wrist and licked my lips. "I promise."

"Say it fully," she ordered me.

"I promise I won't cut myself or take pills again," I said.

When I raised my eyes, I flinched, realizing the guys had all come over and had heard me.

She released me and went into the house, taking her bat with her.

"Maybe you should go," I whispered, still holding my wrist and avoiding looking at their faces.

Kieran walked into the house past me and said, "We haven't had dinner yet."

"The food would go to waste if we left now," Branson said and walked in, too.

"I should check on Sean," I whispered.

Taylor nodded. "I'll go over with you."

We walked side by side in silence. I stepped onto the back porch and all eyes turned to me.

Sean walked over and hugged me immediately. "I'm okay.

He sucker punched me is all." I opened my mouth, and he said, "You better not apologize."

"Don't you worry, Cameron, we'll scare that boy out of town quick," Tamara's dad said. "Creepy ass kid."

"Come here, baby," Tamara's mom said

I walked to her, and she hugged me and pet my hair. "Creepy men are everywhere and pretty girls like you attract them like flies on sugar. It ain't your fault he's following you. You hear me? These boys will keep you safe and if I see him, I'll instill the fear of god into him. No one hurts my girls and you're one of mine now. You hear me?"

I sniffled, trying to keep from crying. "Yes, Ma'am."

"I've already called the sheriff. He said he'd make sure he leaves town," Tamara's dad said.

"You okay?" Wade asked behind me.

"Boy, shut up. No, she is not okay. Some creepy guy just found out where she lives. She is scared and that is perfectly normal. She will be fine, though, because we will ensure he stays away from her," Tamara's mom said.

"Thank you, Goddess," I said to try to ease some of the tension.

She chuckled and patted my head. "Sit down, and I'll get you some of your favorite lemonade."

I nodded and sat on the love seat out of habit.

Sean sat beside me, draped his arm around my shoulders, and pulled me so I rested my head on his shoulder.

"Your nose okay?" I asked.

He nodded. "Yep. It's already stopped bleeding."

"Did you study for math?" Tamara asked.

"Yep!" Taylor answered as he sat on the arm of the love seat next to me. "We studied and I think she's finally ready for the test."

I rolled my eyes. "You're the one who needed the most help."

He scoffed, but didn't deny it.

"Hey, Tamara, you should start coming to our practices with Cameron," Taylor said.

I saw Noah tense in the seat beside me. He hadn't said anything to me or tried to approach me. This weird tension between us was awful and I needed to end it soon.

"No, thank you. Cameron is going to be coming over here and hanging out with me," Tamara said.

"Fine, but only until practice ends," Taylor said. "Then she has to come work out with us. Orders from her Mama."

"What?" Tamara asked, her mouth dropped open. "Seriously?"

I sighed. "Yeah."

"And she has to come to our games, too," Taylor said, smirking.

"Oh, I go to those, too," Tamara said.

"Perfect!" Taylor said. "You guys can watch together."

"Do you even know anything about football?" Noah asked.

I laughed and shook my head. "You throw a ball, catch it and try to cross lines into the touchdown?"

"End zone," Tamara corrected me. "You get a touchdown if you get into the end zone."

My eyes widened. "You know about sports?"

She rolled her eyes. "Girl, we are in the south. Everyone knows about football."

"Plus, her daddy is obsessed with it," Tamara's mom said as she brought Taylor and I glasses of lemonade.

"You'll have to teach me," I said and Tamara smiled with a nod.

"Dinner!" Mama called.

"Take the lemonade and bring me back the glass tomorrow," Tamara's mom said.

"Thank you, Ma'am," Taylor said. "You have the best lemonade in the state."

Tamara's mom giggled. "Oh, go on, you."

"Bye," I said to everyone as I stood, but sat back down and hugged Sean one more time before grabbing Taylor by the elbow. "Come on, Casanova. Let's hurry before the others eat all the food."

He laughed. "That's not necessarily incorrect. They ate all the dinner once while I was in the bathroom."

"They better save me a biscuit," I said with a huff. "Mama's biscuits are delicious."

"Biscuits?" he asked, eyes wide. With a girlish squeal, he sprinted across the grass and into the house. "I heard there were biscuits!" he shouted when he got inside.

I laughed and shook my head. These boys continued to surprise me.

CHAPTER TWELVE

We didn't see Arthur the next few days, and by Friday I felt a little better. Maybe Tamara's dad had scared him enough to stay away.

Mama helped me pack snacks for the meteor shower viewing party with the Gods, and I realized she had even baked biscuits and made jam for us. Or, more accurately, for them.

"You're going to make me look bad if you keep making them treats like this," I warned her.

She laughed. "You'll just have to spend more time in the kitchen until you get as good as me."

"That would likely take the rest of my life," I said and shook my head.

"Don't forget a sweater!" she called after me.

I slid my shoes on and patted my backpack. "Already inside."

"Bug spray? You know how the mosquitos love you."

I nodded. "Sprayed some on already and it's inside, too."

Shoes on, all packed, I turned and smiled at her. "Alright,

I'm off. I'll be back pretty late, but Kieran promised to drive me home."

She nodded. "Keep your guard up. They seem like good boys and have good reputations, but you never know."

I smiled. "Got my mace packed, too."

She laughed. "Good girl. Have fun."

I walked out and waved at Tamara and Sean who were setting up the telescope on her porch.

"Have fun!" Tamara yelled, cupping her hands around her mouth so I heard her.

"You, too!" I called back.

Kieran pulled up in his truck and leaned over to open the passenger door for me. "Ready, Lavender?"

I hopped up into his truck and shut the door. "Yep."

The last few days I'd spent every lunch with them, hung out with Tamara while they practiced, and then went to their house to lift weights. I was incredibly weak, especially compared to them, but they didn't tease me or comment on it. Just showed me the proper way to use the weights and helped me.

Our friendship was definitely growing stronger each day.

I had forgiven Noah and things had returned to normal within our group, including them working with me on my character and teaching me how the game worked before our first planned gaming session the next weekend.

"Seatbelt," Kieran ordered me.

My eyes widened, but I obeyed.

He nodded, satisfied, and put the truck into gear.

"Where are the others?" I asked.

"They're setting up," he said. "Plus, it would be a tight fit with all four of us inside."

I looked out the window. "Oh? I thought maybe you were just trying to get some alone time with me."

He reached over and threaded our fingers together in the center of the bench seat. "There was that, too."

He'd been more affectionate lately, actually all of them had been.

"Are you excited for your game next week?" I asked.

He nodded. "Yeah. It's going to be a lot of fun." He glanced over at me before looking back at the road. "You're coming, right?"

I smiled and squeezed his hand. "I'll be there."

"Good," he said and smirked.

"If you lose, you can't blame me, though," I said.

He laughed. "Why would we blame you?"

"Because it's the first time I'm going and if you lose, it could be that I'm bad luck." Bad luck might as well have been my middle name.

"You're not bad luck, Lavender."

"Mm," I said.

We pulled up to his house, a gorgeous two story with wrap around porches on both floors. His parents sat on the second-floor front porch, on a porch swing, with beers in their hands.

I stepped out of the truck and waved up to them. "Evening!"

"Evening, Cameron," Kieran's mom called down to me.

"Have fun," his dad called.

"We will," Kieran called back, draped an arm around my shoulders and led me around the house towards the back.

"Uh, should you be touching me like this in front of them?" I asked nervously.

He looked down at me and smirked. "They won't care."

"But—"

He leaned down and kissed my burning cheeks. "You're cute when you're flustered."

I huffed and looked away from him. "Whatever."

"There she is!" Branson called out as we rounded the house.

"All set up?" Kieran asked as we joined them beside three motorbikes.

"Uh, what's going on?" I asked nervously.

The three smiled at me.

"We found the perfect spot," Taylor said. "But it's pretty far to walk, so we're going to ride the dirt bikes there."

I eyed them with suspicion. "I can't drive one."

"There's only three," Kieran said. "You'll be riding with one of us."

"Oh," I whispered.

"Don't worry, we've been driving these since we were kids," Branson said.

"Dibs!" Taylor yelled.

"Shit," Branson groaned.

"Dammit," Kieran hissed.

"Uh, what?" I asked.

Taylor pulled me away from Kieran and said, "You're riding with me. I'm the best driver anyway."

"Oh," I whispered.

Honestly, I trusted all three of them, so I wasn't too worried.

"Ready?" he asked.

Nodding, I climbed onto the bike behind him. He showed me where to put my feet and then had me wrap my arms around his waist.

"Don't we need helmets?" I asked over the sounds of the engines.

All three laughed.

"Silly city girl," Taylor said. "No helmets for flat rides when we aren't driving fast."

Oh, good, they wouldn't drive fast.

"Well, not too fast," he said and revved the bike.

I squeaked, which made him laugh.

Kieran took off first, Branson right behind him, and then Taylor followed, but at a much slower pace than the other two.

After a moment, I realized it wasn't so bad and sat up a bit, released my tight hold to a light hold, and looked around the field we drove through.

The sun was already setting and as we drove through the tall grass, hundreds of bugs flew up into the air and started glowing.

I gasped. "Fireflies!"

"Lightning bugs," Taylor corrected. "Wait, have you not seen them before?"

I shook my head and watched the yellow lights flickering around the field.

"Oy!" Taylor yelled. "Detour!"

The two ahead of us turned their bikes in a wide arc, and came up on our sides.

"What's up?" Kieran asked.

Taylor nudged me. "Off the bike, city girl."

Scowling, I climbed off. "Why?"

"She's never seen lightning bugs before," Taylor told the other two as they all put out the bikes' kickstands.

"Really? Even after being here a few weeks?" Branson asked.

I shrugged. "I must have missed them or maybe they just don't like being around my house."

Taylor took my hand and tugged me farther out into the field. "Close your eyes, Cammy."

I tensed. "Why?"

"Please?" he requested.

I sighed, chewed on my lip, but shut them.

We walked for a bit longer. "Sit," he whispered.

"If there's mud or—"

"Just sit," he said with a chuckle.

I sat down and crossed my legs.

"Okay, open your eyes," Taylor said.

I opened my eyes, Branson and Kieran spread their arms out and spun in a few circles in the grass.

Immediately, hundreds of fireflies...lightning bugs...flew up into the sky.

It was one of the most gorgeous sights I had ever seen.

Taylor sat beside me, smiling ear to ear. "So?"

"It's beautiful," I whispered. Wiping my eyes before he could see the happy tears, I leaned over and kissed him. "Thank you."

He brushed my hair behind my ear and smirked. "If I had known showing you bugs would earn me a kiss, I would have done it much sooner."

I laughed and pushed his chest.

He tickled my ribs making me laugh.

I jumped to my feet and ran away. "Hey! No tickling."

The three boys had surrounded me.

"Oh, she's ticklish?" Kieran asked, an evil smirk on his face.

"No, not at all," I lied.

"On three?" Branson asked.

The other two nodded.

I backed up, looking for an escape, but it was too dark, and I didn't really know where to run. "This is not fair. Come on, guys. We're going to miss the meteor shower."

Kieran darted forward, but I spun around his hands with a squeal and started running back towards the bikes.

Branson grabbed me with one arm around my ribs and tickled my stomach with his other hand.

I laughed and kicked, trying to free myself, but he was too strong.

"Give up?" he asked, still tickling me.

I reached back and tickled his stomach, delighted when he yelped and released me.

I turned and wiggled my fingers at him. "Who's ticklish again?"

All three guys froze, and I lunged at Kieran, tickling his stomach and armpits.

He laughed and swatted at my hands.

Out of breath, I sat on my butt and heaved in breaths. "Okay, truce?"

"Out of stamina already?" Kieran asked.

"You would be the first to die in a zombie apocalypse," Branson said and shook his head. "Your mama was right; we do need to work on your stamina."

"Whatever," I said and rolled my eyes.

Taylor held out his hand. "Truce. Let's get to the spot before we do miss the meteor shower."

I climbed onto the bike and hugged him, leaning my head against his back as we finished the drive.

I'd thought it would be a wooden platform, but I hadn't expected it to be a dock out on a pond.

On the dock they had laid out three blankets, an ice chest, a few pillows, and lanterns.

It looked...magical.

"Wow," I whispered.

Taylor waited until I was off the bike before sweeping me up into his arms and holding me against his chest.

I glared at him and threatened, "If you throw me in that water, I will never speak to you ever again."

He rolled his eyes. "I'm not an asshole, Cammy."

"Just had to warn you. I hold grudges, so behave," I said.

"If he throws you in the water, I'll hold him down so you can get some good hits and kicks in, okay?" Kieran promised.

I smiled. "Okay."

"Don't look so excited about beating me up," Taylor said, stuck his lip out in a pout, and continued walking.

I put my arms around his neck and kissed his cheek. "You guys are a lot sweeter and thoughtful than I first thought."

"Anything for you, Cammy," he whispered and kissed me back, this time on the lips.

"Hey! Stop stealing all the time with her!" Branson said.

Taylor smiled, kissed me once more, and carried me over to the dock. He set me in the middle of the blankets, in the center of the dock so I wasn't scared I might fall in the water, and sat down beside me.

I took off my backpack and started pulling out the snacks. "Mama made you guys biscuits and jam."

Three sets of eyes lit up brighter than the bugs and they held out their hands.

Carefully, I buttered and then spread jam on a biscuit for each of them before setting it in their outstretched hands.

They ate them slowly, chewing with closed eyes as they savored the taste.

Jealous of how happy they looked, I made one for myself and agreed, they were delicious.

Branson opened the ice chest and held out a soda to me.

I accepted it with a smile, put it between my crossed legs, and popped the tab to open it.

They took out several different types of snacks, setting them in the middle between all of us.

"How long until the meteors are supposed to show?" I asked.

"Any minute," Taylor said as he messed with his phone.

"Let's put the snacks in the chest so we don't accidentally knock them into the water," Branson suggested.

Knowing me, that is exactly what I would do.

We put everything away, then I lay down in the middle of the blankets and the dock, looking up at the night's sky.

I thought they would lay beside me, but instead, they laid with their heads almost touching mine in a circle.

"Say cheese," Taylor said, held his phone up, and took a picture.

I blinked away the flash's bright light from my eyes.

"Ouch," I said and chuckled.

"There!" Branson called out and raised his arm, pointing at the sky.

We followed the direction of his finger and watched as the meteor shower began.

It was surreal to know those were pieces of a meteor burning up in our atmosphere and we could see them. Back in the city, there were too many lights to be able to view them clearly.

Out here, though, it was easy. There were so many stars out here that weren't visible due to all the light pollution in my last home.

"Thank you," I whispered.

"For what?" Kieran asked.

"For everything," I answered.

"Thank you," Kieran said.

"For what?" I asked, watching the meteor shower triple in size lights flashing all across the sky.

Kieran reached over, linked our hands together and answered, "For existing."

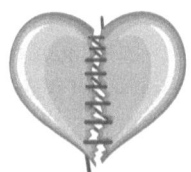

CHAPTER THIRTEEN

The first game was a home game, which everyone said was really good, for some reason.

The Gods had to wear suits all day at school, and at a rally in the cafeteria.

They looked damn good. Too good.

Girls had made signs with the players' names and numbers on them of who they were cheering for.

Of course, over half of them were the Gods'.

In preparation for the night, I re-dyed my hair, keeping it purple at all six of my male friends' requests.

Tamara and I linked arms as we joined the herd of students headed towards the stadium.

"Everyone is really into this," I commented.

She chuckled. "You have no idea."

"Mind if I join you?" Noah asked as he, Wade, and Sean merged into the crowd beside us.

I smiled. "Of course, not! The more the merrier."

"I didn't know you guys were coming," Tamara said, leaning around me to look at them.

"We weren't planning to, but without you two, we weren't going to go sit on your porch," Wade said.

"And we realized we'd rather spend time with you guys, even if it is at a football game," Noah added.

"I'm glad you guys came," I said.

"Are you going to the afterparty?" Sean asked me.

I scowled. "The what?"

"There's always a party after games," Tamara said. "It's an excuse for everyone to blow off steam, get hammered, and hang out. The parents let it happen and the cops wait until close to midnight to break it up."

What a weird town.

"Uh, I don't think I'm going to go to that. I'm not a fan of parties."

"Right," Sean said with a nod. "I forgot about that."

"Did you start reading that book I let you borrow yet?" Wade asked Noah.

Noah shook his head. "I'm finishing up the one Cam let me borrow first."

I groaned. "Hurry up! I want to talk about it."

He laughed. "It's really good. I'm excited to see how it ends."

Clamping my lips together, I held in my evil laughter. I knew how it ended, and he was going to rant and rave for at least two days about it.

"That is not an encouraging look," Noah commented.

"Let's find seats and then a couple of us will go get snacks," Wade said.

"Sounds perfect," I chirped.

We funneled into the entrance, paid our two-dollar entrance fee, and then we let the guys lead us to seats.

Once seated, Sean, Wade, and Noah took our orders and cash, and went off to buy the food.

"You didn't make a sign?" Tamara teased as we saw Sylvia and her cronies each with signs.

I rolled my eyes. "No. No, I did not."

We both laughed and shook our heads.

"Why do you think she's so stuck on them?" I asked Tamara softly.

She looked at me with an arched brow. "Like you aren't?"

I scowled at her. "No. We're friends, but I'm still leaving at the end of the school year."

It was her turn to scowl. "So, if one of them asked you to stay and live with them, you wouldn't?"

"I know where I'm moving," I whispered and looked out over the crowd gathering in the stands. "And it's not here."

"Ouch," she whispered.

I hugged her. "I'm telling you, we can alter my plan so you can come with me."

She patted my arm. "Thanks, but I've got my plan." She looked behind me, and I turned to find her boyfriend coming down the stairs towards us.

"Oh! That's why you come to the games," I realized. "Sneaky girl."

She chuckled. "Guilty as charged."

He sat down and kissed her cheek, then leaned around her to smile at me. "Hi, Cameron."

"Hey," I said.

"Cameron, this is Mike. Mike this is Cameron." Tamara's smile was infectious.

I held out my hand and he shook it.

"Hey, Mikey is here!" Wade said as he sat in front of us, his hands full of bagged treats.

Once he set the treats on the bleachers beside him, he and Mike bumped fists.

"Hey, Mike." Sean nodded towards him, arms full. He sat

beside me and I took a few of the things he had to lighten is haul.

"Hey, Sean. How's that campaign going?" Mike asked.

"Pretty good. I got all the maps drawn and everything," Sean said. "We're going to start playing it next weekend, actually. You want to join?"

"I'd love to," Mike said. "I already have a character ready to go."

Sean laughed. "I bet you've got a handful ready to go."

"Guilty as charged!" Mike said.

Sean and Mike laughed together and I felt somewhat sure I knew what they were talking about, but also not one hundred percent certain.

"Cam is going to play with us this time," Sean said.

"Oh?" Mike asked and looked at me. "You play Beasts and Bossfights?"

"I will next weekend!" I said.

Everyone laughed.

"I got you a pretzel, since I know you like them," Noah said and held a large, salted soft pretzel out to me.

My mouth dropped, and I gasped excitedly. "Oh, my gosh. I haven't had one of these in years."

"I got you mustard and nacho cheese sauce because I didn't know which you wanted," Noah added and handed me two cups of yellow deliciousness.

I squealed. "You rock."

Mike chatted with the other guys about Beasts and Bossfights.

Tamara leaned over and whispered, "This is why I was so excited you were coming, too. I'm often left out of the conversations because I don't play."

"Well, you're going to have to spend most of the game explaining it to me, so we'll be busy," I said.

She laughed. "You got it."

The announcer started introducing the teams and saying stuff that made no sense to me, but then our team ran out onto the field and everyone cheered. I cheered with them.

I spotted the guys easily, a smile splitting my face instantly.

"Don't look so excited," Tamara teased me.

Sylvia and her cronies stood and screamed the Gods' names.

It felt like an hour before the game finally started. Once it did, I was completely lost. Tamara tried to explain things to me, and I got a few things, but downs made no sense and neither did when they turned the ball over to the other side if no one had scored a touchdown yet.

At the end of the game, our team won by a landslide.

I wanted to congratulate the guys, but I knew they were likely to get cornered and bombarded from other people who had watched.

We walked out of the stadium, and I sent the guys text messages congratulating them.

I bumped into someone as I was texting, and almost dropped my phone.

"Oh, I'm so sorry," I said and raised my head to look at the person.

Our eyes connected, my lungs froze, and it felt like my heart stopped.

Victoria, leader of the gang from my last school, and the one who had used me as bait stood in front of me. She wore a pair of tight pants, a tank top that showed off her arm muscles, and her normal combat boots. Her long, thick hair was braided down her back, but there was no dyed color in it like she normally had. "Hey, chick!"

She moved towards me like she was going to touch me, and

I jumped back, bumping into Sean and Wade behind me, making us all stumble.

She smiled. "Ah, come on. You aren't still upset about last year, are you? Water under the bridge, right homegirl?"

"Wh-why are you here? How are you h-here? What?" I stammered.

"What's going on?" Sean asked me.

"I need to go. We need to go," I said urgently.

"Oh, but we haven't caught up yet! I hear you've got a lot going on at this school already. Come on, come talk to me," she said and grabbed my wrist.

I jerked my wrist out of her hold and shook my head. "N-no. Just leave. Leave me alone."

Victoria tsked. "You're not being nice to your best friend."

"You have no idea what a f-friend is!" I yelled at her. "You bitch!"

Her face hardened. "It's not nice to call names, Camerolina."

I flinched at the old nickname. "I'm sorry. Please, just leave me alone."

Tamara walked over, smiling wide, grabbed my arm, and pulled me into the crowd. "Hurry up or we'll miss our ride," she said way too cheerfully for her usual self.

Wade and Noah stepped behind me quickly so Victoria couldn't grab me.

"I'll see you soon, Camerolina. You can't hide from me," Victoria called after me.

First Arthur and now her? How the hell had she found me? And why? Why was she so far from home?

"Noah," I whispered as he came up to my side.

He put his arm around my waist. "You're alright. We've got you. You're not going to faint. There's no danger."

"Danger. Sh-she's dangerous," I said.

"Get her in the truck," Sean said.

"Sleepover?" Tamara asked.

Sean said something, but I was already falling unconscious.

"Cam?" Tamara asked, her voice distorted. "She's fainted."

Hands moved me, but I knew these people were safe at least.

Time became disjointed, and when I finally regained control, we were on Tamara's porch and I was lying on the love seat.

"There she is," Noah said softly and brushed my hair out of my face.

"D-did she f-follow?"

He shook his head. "No. We're safe."

I cried and leaned up to hug him.

He held me as I cried, petting my hair. "It'll be okay."

Nothing was okay.

"Where is she?" Kieran asked.

"In the back," Sean answered.

Noah helped me sit up and then Taylor squatted between my legs and stared into my eyes. "Talk to us."

"She's the one wh-who used me as b-bait," I stammered, tears streaming down my face.

"She's from California?" Taylor asked and I nodded.

"How the hell did she find her out here?" Kieran asked.

"I don't know. I deleted BookFace and everything," I said.

"No, you didn't," Branson said.

I looked over at him. "What?"

"Your BookFace is still up. I tagged you in that picture we took the night of the meteor shower," he said.

Everyone came to the same conclusion at the same time.

"Shit," Branson said. "I'm sorry, Cam. I didn't know you weren't using it. I mean, I saw that you hadn't posted recently, but I didn't realize you'd uninstalled it and weren't using it."

"I said to delete it," I whispered. "I told the app to delete the profile."

"The app never deletes a profile," Sean said. "You have to go in and change the settings to completely private in order to make it unviewable."

Dammit, I hadn't known that.

"Why would she come all the way out here?" Kieran asked me.

Honestly, I didn't know. It's not like I owed her anything.

I shook my head. "I don't know."

As I thought about it, I realized the Gods were here.

I looked up at them. "You're here? Why? The afterparty?"

Taylor wiped the tears from my face and smiled sweetly. "We can go to parties whenever we want. Come on, Cammy, you know you're more important to us."

"What's going on?" Tamara's mom asked.

Looking around, I saw all of the concerned faces of my friends. True friends who wanted to protect me, to help me, to be my friends no matter what had happened to me in the past. They didn't care if I was cool, acted tough, or forced me to prove my loyalty. They loved me for me.

"Nothing," I said, stood and wiped my face. "I need to get home."

These people were good people. They didn't need to be involved in my drama. This was my problem. My trouble. My bad decisions that had followed me.

It was up to me to fix it myself.

Either I stayed the scared little bitch I was or I handled my shit. It was time to suck it up and handle my shit.

Noah grabbed my wrist. "You're not going to run from us."

I smiled and kissed his cheek. "I'm not running. Not anymore."

CHAPTER FOURTEEN

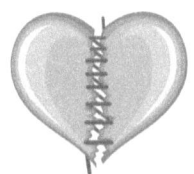

It took me a little bit of time to log back into my BookFace account, but once I had, it was easy to find Victoria's profile. I sent her a message, gave her an address, and told her to meet me there at eleven o'clock. Not even a minute later she messaged back a smiley face and agreed to meet.

Since I didn't want to endanger anyone, I packed my bag, got dressed, and as soon as Mama fell asleep, snuck out of the house.

I made it past Tamara's house before I gained a follower.

Groaning, I turned and crossed my arms over my chest. "Why are you following me?"

Sean and Noah stepped out of the shadows.

"We figured you were planning something stupid, and we wanted to make sure we followed you in case you did," Sean said.

"This is something I have to do. Alone," I told them.

"That's not how friendship works," Kieran said from behind me.

I screeched, my hand flying to my pounding heart as I turned to face him. "You three, too?"

"Where are you going, Cammy?" Taylor asked, scowling at me.

"Please, stay away. I've caused you all so much trouble and I'm done. I can't do this anymore. I can't be this pathetic little shell that I am and continue hurting you all and causing trouble. This is my problem and I am going to fix it," I said sternly, turned, and walked through the towering flesh walls that were the Gods.

"Okay," Branson said and walked beside me.

I looked over at him. "What?"

He smiled, linked his hands behind his back, and said, "You want to handle this by yourself and I get that. So, we'll let you handle it, but we're still coming."

I groaned. "You can't be with me. She's not going to talk to me if you're there."

"She won't see us," Noah said. "We know this town better than anyone. We'll hide nearby so we can keep an eye on you while you talk to her."

"You don't even know where I'm meeting her," I said, turning to walk backwards so I could look at the guys following me.

"The park," all five said at the same time.

My mouth dropped.

"It's the only place you could meet her that won't have people at it and is far enough away you thought you could hide from us," Kieran said.

"Are you armed?" Taylor asked me.

I chuckled. "With mace."

All five scowled at me.

"I'm not using a gun!" Shaking my head, I turned back around to face the direction I was walking. The last thing I needed was to knock myself out walking.

"What if she has a gun?" Kieran asked.

I shrugged. "I've been shot before."

Kieran grabbed my wrist, pulling me to a stop and spun me around so I faced him. He tilted my face up so I had to meet his eyes and said, "Don't be so quick to offer up your life. You mean a lot to a lot of people."

Taking the hand on my chin, I slid it up to my cheek, resting my face against it. "Don't worry, I'm not going to offer up my life so easily."

"Promise?" he whispered.

I nodded. "Promise."

He kissed me and before he could say anything else, I spun and ran down the sidewalk.

There was no one walking about or driving, and all of the stores were closed.

The park only had a couple of lights on, but it was easy to spot Victoria. She sat on one of the tables, flipping a knife in her hand.

She was always one for the dramatic and loved to show off how tough she was.

"Oy," I called out to her as I approached.

She flipped her blade closed and stood, putting her hands in her pockets. "You showed. I'm honestly surprised."

"What do you want, Victoria? Why did you travel so far to see me? I don't have anything you want so why are you here?" The questions tumbled out one after the other and I clamped my lips shut afterwards to stop talking.

"Where did you hide the stash?" she asked me.

I blinked a few times in stunned silence. "What stash?"

She drew the blade and pressed it to my throat. "The drugs you stole from them when you went in as bait!" she yelled.

I held up my hands. "I didn't take anything from them. You saw what condition I was in. I never even made it into their house. They snatched me from the porch."

"They killed Anton! They said you stole from them!" she screamed.

Anton had been her lover, one of them anyway.

"I did not take anything from them. They are lying to you and just using me as a scapegoat. I haven't done drugs since the night before I went to them. The night before you used me as fucking bait. So, if you don't have anything else to say to me, get out of my town and don't come back. I've given up a life of drugs and crime. I don't want to be involved in your dirty business anymore."

She unfolded the knife with a flick of her wrist and pressed the tip of the knife into my throat in one smooth motion. The sting let me know it was drawing blood. "Don't lie to me, hoe! Where did you hide it? They said you hid it at our place!"

"You can't be this stupid," I said and scoffed. "They're lying to you. You left your place unguarded? You're going to get home and everyone is going to be dead because you let them get to you. They just proved they're a better gang than yours. You just lost."

"I haven't lost anything!" she screamed at me.

"I'm sorry. I don't have anything to offer you. I didn't steal from them. There is nothing that I hid at your place. If you remember, after they beat the shit out of me I went to the hospital, went to school and you told me I was trash and beat me up some more, and I never went back to your house. So, there's no way I could have left anything there."

She screamed and pressed the knife deeper. "You're lying."

"You know I'm not. I may have been a lot of things while I hung out with you, but I was never a liar," I whispered.

She withdrew the knife and then punched me. "Why are you acting like a fucking goody two-shoes? What happened to Camerolina? You were so tough and fierce. Where is she?"

I rubbed my chin and said. "She died the night I tried to

take my life after you told me I was trash because the people you used me as bait for raped me."

She spit to the right. "You are trash."

I straightened and said, "No, I'm not. It took me moving to this BFE town to realize that I am not trash. I am not worthless. I am a human and I deserve to be happy. So do you, Vicky. Stop playing gangster and live your life. You only get one."

"Fuck you. You don't know me!" she spat.

"I do," I said. "I know you better than anyone else. I spent the most time with you when you were too trashed to walk. I heard all the things you cried about in secret. You don't have to hide in the shadows. You don't have to pretend to be tough. You are pretty. You are smart. You could do anything you wanted. Leave that shithole of a town and go out on your own. Find love. You can. It's possible."

"You found love, huh?" she asked and scoffed. "In this dump?"

I shrugged. "Maybe. It's way too early for me to know, but I have found friends and that's good enough for me. I'd rather have friends than people who use me."

She shoved me and stalked away. "Whatever, loser. Stay here in your cowdung shit hole and rot."

It wasn't until Noah picked me up in his arms that I realized I had fallen to my knees in the cold grass.

"She's gone?" I asked.

He nodded, his jaw tight.

"What's wrong?" I asked.

"You're bleeding."

I touched my throat. "I'm okay."

Noah set me down, and Sean hurried over, inspecting the wound, cleaning it, and then bandaging it. "She's okay," he told the others who crowded around us.

I was okay and for the first time, I felt...free.

Laughter bubbled up in my chest and then spilled out uncontrollably. I laughed until my stomach hurt and beyond, clutching it tightly.

"She go insane?" Branson asked.

I nodded and wiped my eyes. "Probably."

"Come on, let's get you home," Kieran said and helped me stand up.

I walked amongst my guys and said, "It's going to be really hard to leave at the end of the school year."

"Why don't you stay then?" Branson suggested.

I shook my head. "I can't. I have a place to go." But maybe, just maybe, I could convince some of them to go with me. Not yet, though.

"So, how did you enjoy your first football game?" Taylor asked me.

I shrugged. "It was okay. I didn't understand what the heck was going on the first quarter, but Tamara explained it as we went along and I started picking it up. You guys stomped on that other team."

"Yeah, we did," Taylor said and he, Kieran, and Branson high-fived each other.

"So modest," I teased.

"What are you doing tomorrow?" Sean asked.

I shrugged. "I don't have plans."

"Want to go to some garage sales?" he asked. "Not the rummage sale," he quickly added.

I nodded. "That sounds awesome. I need some more books."

"Didn't you just get a tote of books?" Kieran asked.

I nodded. "Yeah, but I'll finish those pretty soon so I need more."

"She already finished half of them," Sean told them.

I smacked his arm. "Don't tell them how nerdy I am."

Kieran put his arm around my waist and pulled me against his side as we walked. "We already know, Lavender. We already know."

"Hey, why don't you guys join us next weekend?" Sean suggested. "I think you guys would make great players."

"What's next weekend?" Branson asked, his eyes wide with curiosity.

"We play this game called Beasts and Bossfights. You create a character and then fight creatures and search for treasures," Noah explained.

"Can I create a barbarian?" Branson asked.

I laughed. "You're definitely a tank."

"Tank?" Branson asked.

As we finished our walk, Sean and Noah told them all about Beasts and Bossfights. Much to my surprise, they agreed to come the next weekend to play.

I said goodnight to the Gods, Noah, and then made Sean wait a second.

"What?" he asked.

"You don't have to invite them if you don't want," I whispered.

He smiled. "I invited them because I thought it would be more fun with them there. And, I think they would have a lot of fun. They're all a crazy group of characters, and I know that at least Branson will get into it, especially the role-playing part."

"Thank you," I whispered.

"For what?" he asked.

"For being you," I said, wrapped my arms around his neck, and kissed him.

He wrapped his arms around me, pulled me flush against his body, and kissed me back.

When we separated, I was panting.

"I need to get home," he said. "I've got to open the store."

I nodded, but pulled him back for another kiss.

He chuckled as we kissed, but kissed me back.

"Goodnight," I said and forced myself to separate from him and walk up my porch steps.

"Goodnight, my goddess," he said.

I turned around to say something, my mouth open, but he was already jogging across the grass.

"Have an interesting night?" Mama asked behind me.

I cringed and turned around slowly. "Yeah."

She held open the door for me. "You're grounded for a week."

I bowed my head as I walked by. "Yes, ma'am."

"And next time you go to face off with a gang member, take my bat with you, okay?"

I spun around, mouth open. "You knew?"

She smirked. "Who do you think called the Gods?" Before I could answer, she swatted my butt. "Get to bed."

Sleep was the furthest thing from my mind as I went upstairs and lay on my bed.

Finally, after all that had happened, I had regained a bit of myself. Standing up to her had been terrifying, but now that I had done it I felt a little less terrified of the world.

As much as I wanted to chalk it up to my own lessons learned, it was one hundred percent because of my friends here. None of this would have happened without them.

Kieran: You still awake?

Me: You know it.

Kieran: You okay?

Me: Yes.

Kieran: Good. I almost charged out there when she put that knife to your throat, but the others held me back.

Me: I'm glad you didn't come out.

Kieran: Are you okay with us coming next weekend?

Me: 100%

Kieran: Okay. We don't want to intrude, but we want to know more about you and thought this was the best way.

Me: You sure you'll be able to handle others knowing you're playing a geeky game like Beasts and Bossfights?

Kieran: As long as it means spending time with you, I'd even paint my nails.

Me: Don't make promises you won't keep.

Kieran: As long as it's a color I pick...

Me: Neon pink

Kieran: Veto

Me: Purple

Kieran: Veto

Me: Midnight blue

Kieran: ...maybe

Me: What are your plans after the school year?

It occurred to me that I hadn't even asked them yet. I didn't know if they were going to college, trying to get a football scholarship, or starting work at a family business, or anything. I had no idea.

Kieran: All we know is that we want to leave this town. Aside from that, Branson, Taylor, and I are going to stick together and that's all we care about.

Me: You aren't going to play football?

Kieran: No. There's too many cases of people becoming permanently injured at a young age. I'd rather be healthy and happy than rich.

Me: I'd rather you didn't get injured, either.

Kieran: Are you insinuating that you might want to see me after high school?

Me: Don't push your luck. I haven't known you that long yet.

Kieran: It doesn't feel that way, though, does it? I feel like I've known you my whole life.

Me: Same.

I chewed on my lip after responding, unsure what to do next. Admitting how close I felt to them so soon wasn't something I had planned. Keeping it secret was my intention.

Kieran: Don't worry, Lavender, I won't make you choose between me and the others. I know your heart isn't ready for that.

He wasn't wrong. My heart was really really confused at the moment with so many guys around me. I wasn't stupid enough to think that I was in love with any of them, but my feelings were definitely more than friendly and I had them for all of them.

He said he wouldn't make me choose now, but I didn't doubt that by the end of the school year he would.

Of course, by that time, I likely would have chosen myself. Or, I hoped so. I didn't want to be that slut who tried to keep all the boys to herself.

Me: I appreciate that. I also appreciate you being there for me so often this school year. I feel like I owe you.

Kieran: You could bake me something.

Me: HAHA. I could have Mama bake you something

Kieran: NOPE. Has to be from you. I don't care if it's terrible. You bake it and I will eat it.

Me: If you die from salmonella poisoning, you can't blame me.

Kieran: Noted.

Me: Deal.

We continued talking until my eyes got too heavy and my thumbs stopped writing the correct words. Once we said goodnight, I fell into a deep sleep.

That deep sleep was broken by something hitting my window.

I rolled out of bed with a groan, walked down the stairs, out of my house, and around the side of my house while rubbing my eyes. "I just fell asleep, Kieran. What are you doing—"

"Who's Kieran?" Arthur asked.

My eyes snapped open and I froze. I hadn't looked outside because I'd thought it would be Kieran.

Arthur walked closer, smiling wide. "I like your pajamas."

Hurrying backwards I asked, "What are you doing here?"

He scowled. "I heard someone hurt you earlier." His eyes zeroed in on my throat. "Was it one of those guys?"

My phone was up in my room, I wore just light pajama pants and a tank top with a sports bra. There was literally nothing on me that I could use to protect myself.

"Please leave," I said.

"But I came all this way to see you," he said happily. "I know this spot where they serve breakfast all night long. Come on, I'll take you."

I shook my head and backed up. "No, you need to leave."

"No, I don't. Come on, I'll pay for the food," he said and reached out towards me.

I spun away from him and screamed.

He put one hand over my mouth and the other arm he wrapped around my waist. "Hey, stop screaming. You're going to wake people up."

He had cupped his hand so I couldn't bite him and no matter how hard I struggled, he didn't let go.

"Why are you being so obstinate?" he asked. "Just let me take you out for food."

I screamed as loud as I could around his hand, but it wasn't loud enough. Kicking his shins didn't do anything either and he just picked me up off the ground.

"Oh, you're sleep walking!" he exclaimed. "That makes sense. I'll knock you out and when you wake up, we'll be at breakfast. Don't worry."

I screamed when he let go of my mouth, but then his fist hit the back of my head, making the stars spin, and no matter how hard I tried, I couldn't keep my eyes open.

CHAPTER FIFTEEN

Waking up in a stalker's car was bad enough, but waking up with my hands tied behind my back, a rag in my mouth, and my feet bound was even worse.

I screamed and tried to get the door open, but the seatbelt was on and I couldn't get out.

"Whoa, easy," Arthur said and chuckled. "You could have fallen out. I'm glad I tied you up. Silly sleepwalker."

If I didn't get free, I didn't want to think about what he might do. I had to break free, get a phone, and call for help.

"We're almost there," he said. "They have the best pancakes in three counties. You'll love them. I recommend the scrambled eggs, too."

Struggling would get me nowhere except to use up all my energy, so I relaxed on the seat and looked at the scenery around us.

Nothing looked familiar. How far had he taken me? The sun was rising, so it was at least four hours later.

He reached over and tugged on a bit of my hair. "The purple is super pretty. It made it a lot easier to find you. I'd probably still be searching the state to try to find you if it weren't for this."

Taking deep breaths to keep calm, I took stock of everything. The ropes around my wrists were tight, so I couldn't untie them. The ones on my ankles were looser, but without the use of my hands, it was still pointless. The gag in my mouth was loose, but not loose enough to get out.

If he really was just taking me to a meal at a restaurant, then I would have a chance to escape when he untied me. If he lied and was taking me to his house...I would have to figure out what to do then.

"Those guys you were with...they seem like jerks. Were they just bothering you and you didn't want to tell me?" He looked at me, but I kept my gaze away from his. "Yeah, that's probably it. Guys like that don't know when to take no for an answer."

Oh, that was rich coming from him!

"Don't worry, I won't let them deter me. I could tell that you and I had chemistry instantly. There's a spark between us that demands we see it out," he continued.

Gag me with a spoon. No, thank you.

"Here we are!" he said as he pulled off the road, into a dirt parking lot of a restaurant. There were two other cars there, which I was fairly certain were people who worked there.

Once parked, he untied me.

Free, I opened the door slowly, waiting until he started unbuckling himself and opened his door before I ran as fast as I could off into the woods.

"Hey!" he called and chased after me.

Crying would only hinder my view, so I fought back the tears and focused on fleeing. My only chance was to get as far from him as I could.

"Are you sleep-running?" he called from far too close to me.

"It's dangerous to run off into the woods out here. A bear might get you."

Looking back at him was not an option. I ran as fast as my legs would take me, glad for the endurance training the guys had started giving me and wishing we had done more at the same time.

Swerving amongst the trees, I veered towards the road, hoping someone might see me and stop to help.

Large hands grabbed my shoulders just as the road came into sight, halting me. "Whoa! You almost ran out into the road! That is super dangerous."

"Let me go!" I screamed. "Stop touching me!"

"It's okay, it's just me," Arthur said. "I'm not going to hurt you."

"Leave me alone, freak!" I screamed and kicked him in the shin as hard as I could.

He grunted, but his fingers dug into my shoulders so hard that I cried out in pain. "That hurt! Why are you acting so crazy? Do you need a hospital? Are you an escaped psychiatric patient?"

What the hell was wrong with this guy? He kidnapped me from my house and then tried to say I was an escaped psychiatric patient? I knew he was a few marbles short of a bag, but this...

"Fuck off!" I screamed at him, spun under his arms, and punched him as hard as I could in the stomach.

He gasped as my hit went a little high, hitting his sternum instead of chest. "Ouch. Why are you being so mean?"

"Leave me alone!" I screamed and ran back towards the restaurant. If I could get inside and use their phone, I could call someone.

I made it into the restaurant and ran behind the counter.

The waitress's mouth dropped open. "What are you doing?" she gasped.

"This crazy guy kidnapped me," I told her and dropped to the ground so if he came inside, he wouldn't see me. "Please, help me."

She looked towards the door and frowned. "Shit, it's Arthur again, isn't it?"

I nodded. "I'm new to Sheldon and I ran into him at a rummage sale. Please. Please don't tell him I'm here. Please help me. I just need to call a friend to come get me."

She kept her eyes on the door. "Don't worry, honey. We've dealt with this before." She grabbed a cordless phone from the wall and held it out to me.

I quickly dialed Kieran's number. It took five rings before he answered, his voice groggy, "Hello?"

"Help!" I hissed. "Arthur kidnapped me and took me to..." I looked up at the waitress.

She took the phone and told Kieran the name and address of the restaurant.

"Hurry," I begged him.

"We're on our way," he assured me, noise in the background.

I hung up, and she put the phone on the receiver.

The front door opened, and I curled up tighter, clenching my eyes closed to keep from seeing him.

"Did a girl run in here? I think she might be a psychiatric patient that escaped," Arthur said, his voice out of breath.

"Sorry, but no one's come in here except you this morning," the waitress lied with a smile.

"Oh, weird. I thought I saw her run in here," Arthur said.

"Have you checked the store down the street?" she asked. "I know people like to run there from time to time."

"Right! Thanks. I always forget about the store! I'll find her and bring her back for pancakes!" he yelled and left.

I still didn't move. My eyes clenched tightly closed as tears leaked onto the floor below me.

"He's gone," she whispered, "but it's probably best not to have you in sight just in case he returns. Your friend will be here soon."

"Thank you," I gasped out as she helped me stand and into the back where a tiny office that could only fit a desk and chair.

She helped me to the chair and then brought me a cup of hot chocolate. "Just sit tight, honey."

I nodded numbly and sipped on the hot chocolate.

Time passed strangely as I waited, still worried he might show up and grab me.

When the door flung open, I screamed and threw my cup toward it.

Thankfully, it hit the wall beside the door and not the person in the doorway.

Taylor ran to me and hugged me, tucking my head against his chest. "It's okay, Cammy. We're here."

I cried and clung to him. "He took me and I didn't have my phone and he tied me up and—"

"Shh, it's okay, baby girl, we're here. You're safe," he whispered.

"She's in here?" an older male voice asked.

"Yes, sir," the waitress said.

Taylor turned so I could look at the door at the man in a police uniform in the doorway. He was well into his sixties, his belly hanging over the top of his pants and his button-up shirt barely able to stay closed.

"You say he kidnapped you?" he asked.

I nodded and wiped my face on my hands. "Yes, sir. He came to my house and I thought it was my friends throwing rocks at my window, but it was him. He grabbed me and wouldn't take no for an answer. I tried to escape, but he said he thought I was sleep-walking and tied me up and knocked me out."

The officer sighed. "That boy has always been trouble, but this is the last straw. Did he hurt you?"

I shook my head. "No, sir."

He nodded. "Alright. Write down your address and home phone on this paper, and I'll let your friends take you home."

He held out a pad of paper, and I wrote my information down with shaking hands.

Taylor kept his arm around me as we walked out of the restaurant and out to Kieran's truck.

He and Branson rushed over after talking to a female officer, hugging me around Taylor.

I cried again, fresh tears coming.

"It's okay," Branson whispered. "It's okay."

"Let's get in the truck and get her home," Taylor said softly.

Kieran climbed into the driver's seat, Taylor shoved me over beside Kieran, Branson climbed in next, and Taylor sat against the door.

It was a really tight fit, so Kieran grabbed my legs and draped them over his right leg. Branson tucked me close against his side, putting an arm around my waist, and buckled us into one seat belt.

Once on the road, I leaned my face into the crook of Branson's upper arm and closed my eyes.

"Did...did he touch you?" Kieran asked, and I heard the steering wheel creak as his grip tightened.

I shook my head, but refused to open my eyes.

"That's good," Branson said and pet my hair. "Real good."

"Yeah, otherwise we'd have to kill him," Taylor said, but there was zero teasing in his tone.

"Mama..." I choked on the word.

"We called her," Branson said. "She was too scared to drive well, and we promised to deliver you straight to her."

"How f-far?" I asked.

"A couple of hours. You should try to sleep," Kieran said and stroked one of my legs.

"We've got you, Cammy. You're safe here," Taylor whispered.

New tears came and I couldn't stop them no matter how hard I tried.

The guys pet me as we drove, lapsing into silence. What was there to say? Once again, I had called on them to rescue me. Once again, I had forced them to drive and find me.

"I'm sorry," I whispered. "Thank you for coming. I'm sorry you had to drive so far and—"

"Don't apologize," Branson said sternly. "You have nothing to apologize for."

"I keep making you go out of your way and—"

"Did you call him? Did you climb into his truck? Did you ask to come to this restaurant?" Kieran asked.

"No," I whispered.

He threaded one set of his fingers through mine. "Then you didn't do anything."

"You called your friends for help," Taylor whispered and kissed the top of my head. "I'm glad we were able to help you. I only wish we had been here sooner."

"Will he come again?" I asked. People weren't in jail very long, even for heinous crimes.

"We called our sheriff and he is going to come by the house to get your statement and confirm the guy's identity. Once he does that, there will be a city-wide notice that he is not allowed to enter our city boundaries and if he does, the cops will immediately be called and they'll escort him out," Taylor said.

"Don't I need to file a restraining order for that?" I asked.

"No, not here," Kieran said. "Things are run differently here."

"Close your eyes," Branson whispered. "Rest."

I closed my eyes, snuggled between them with their caresses constant and soft, reassuring me.

Fate wasn't something I believed in. Neither was love at first sight or soul mates. However, I did feel like meeting these three was meant to be. Like our friendship was something stronger than normal.

"I'm going to bake you guys treats," I mumbled as I started to drift off.

"Oh? What kind?" Kieran asked softly.

"Cookies," I said. "I don't know what kind, but...cookies."

"We love cookies," Branson said.

"I love our friendship," I whispered.

"What?" Kieran asked.

I didn't respond, my body choosing that moment to descend into blissful sleep.

"Why are they flat?" I screeched as I pulled out my second tray of cookies from the oven.

Mom chuckled. "Oh, honey. You really are hopeless."

Branson snatched a cookie off the tray, blowing on it and switching it quickly between each of his hands since it was so hot. He took a bite and moaned. "It tastes delicious."

"You said that about the last batch and they were under-cooked," I reminded him, smirking.

"Who doesn't love chewy cookies?" Taylor asked and stole the second half of the cookie from Branson. He chewed on it and moaned. "So good."

"I think what the boys are trying to tell you is that it tastes good because you made it with love," Mom said, smiling sweetly.

I felt my cheeks warm and turned back to the oven to prepare the next tray to go inside. "Right," I whispered.

"What are you kids up to after she finishes baking?" Mom asked.

"We're taking her dirt bike riding," Taylor said.

"Oh? I didn't know you enjoyed that," Mom said.

I shrugged. "I didn't either until they forced me on one."

"Where are you going riding?" she asked.

"Just on my property," Kieran answered. "We have a trail that we've created over the years. No jumps or anything like that."

"Keep her safe," she said and walked out of the kitchen. "I've got plans with my girlfriends. Call my cell if you need me."

Everyone said bye to her.

My entire body tensed as I realized she had left me alone with three boys in the house.

"She must really trust you guys," I whispered, opened the oven, and slid the cookie tray inside.

After shutting the door and setting the timer, I turned around and found three cocky smiles on their faces.

"Did you know that she told us we could date you?" Taylor asked.

I rolled my eyes. "No, she didn't. Mama wouldn't give three guys the option to date me."

"She did," Branson said and made an X on his chest.

"She's against polygamy," I informed them.

"We didn't say marry you," Kieran said and smirked. "But good to know you've discussed that with her before."

My face was on fire as I gaped at him. "I, uh..."

"Knock, knock!" Sean called out as he simultaneously knocked and opened the door.

"In the kitchen!" Taylor called out.

Sean came inside, his button-up shirt sleeves were rolled up, exposing his tattoos. When he came in the kitchen, I immediately hugged him.

He kissed my cheek and then swiped a cookie from the cooling tray. "Oh, cookies?"

"Hey, those are ours!" Branson cried out.

Sean popped the full cookie in his mouth and chewed it up with a glint in his eyes. When he finished he said, "These are good. You used too much butter, though."

I blinked. "What?"

"That's why they're flat," he explained. "Too much butter."

"You...bake?" I asked.

He smiled. "Yes."

"Could...would you teach me?" I asked.

He nodded. "Sure."

"Only if we get to sample everything," Taylor said quickly.

Sean rolled his eyes. "Like I could get rid of you three if I tried."

"I mean, you could try, but I wouldn't suggest it," Kieran said.

If it weren't for the way they were smiling at each other, I would be nervous they were about to fight.

"Are you going to bring some of these tonight?" Sean asked, turning back to me.

"I can make another batch," I said, but looking at the time I realized I didn't have long before our game session. "Or..."

"We can bring most of these," Kieran said, "but we get to keep some for ourselves."

Sean shrugged. "You don't have to bring them. It was just a suggestion."

"Are you excited?" I asked him.

He nodded. "This is the first time we've had a group this large, and I can't wait to see these three joining in the game."

"I watched some videos of people playing and I'm so ready to play," Branson said. "I was thinking about giving my character an accent."

I laughed. "You have an accent."

He rolled his eyes. "No, you have an accent. You're the only one here who sounds different."

"No, people from California just don't have an accent. You just drop your accent to sound Californian," I argued.

"Whatever," Branson said in his best California voice. It was actually pretty good.

"That was kind of hot," I told him and giggled. "Okay, I have to clean up and change before we go."

"We'll help," Kieran said.

"You don't have to," I told them, but they were already throwing trash away and grabbing the broom and dust pan.

I grabbed the bowls and spoons, taking them to the sink to wash.

"I'll help," Sean said, coming up beside me.

"Thanks," I replied, smiling up at him.

I washed and he dried, which made it a quick operation.

By the time we were done, the other three had finished cleaning the rest of the kitchen and had even bagged up the cookies into five bags.

"Why five?" I asked curiously.

"One for each of us," Kieran said and gestured to all of us.

I leaned up and kissed his cheek. "You're so considerate."

"Go change," he said. "Or I'll make you go with flour in your hair."

I stuck my tongue out at him and then ran up the stairs to my room. One look in the mirror confirmed he hadn't been lying about the flour in my hair. It was in my hair, on my face, my arms, and all over my clothes.

It looked like I'd had a flour fight instead of baking some cookies.

Thankfully, I had already spent the previous night picking out my outfit, even had Tamara's help choosing just the right one.

Since we were going to nerd out, I put on a pair of black yoga pants, an oversized t-shirt that hung low enough to cover my butt if it wasn't tied, which it currently was, and flip flops. With the little time I had, I was only able to rinse my face and put some eyeshadow, mascara, and eyeliner on.

As I reached for my hairbrush, I glanced at the window that was now locked closed and covered. Kieran had insisted that I do it, to make him feel better. I hadn't argued.

I quickly brushed out my hair and left it down. If I braided it, Kieran would untie it and let the braid loose.

Satisfied with my appearance, I skipped down the stairs and back into the kitchen where the four guys were whispering with fierce expressions.

"What's wrong?" I asked.

All four turned around and took a moment to look me up and down.

Score one for Tamara's suggestion on super casual.

"Nothing," Sean said and smiled wide. "You ready to go?"

"Where are we going?" I asked.

"The store," he said. "It's closed early today so we can use the backroom."

"Really? The owner lets you do that?" I asked.

"Well, it is my uncle that owns it," Sean said. "So, I get special privileges."

"Oh," I said. That was information I probably knew and forgot. Or, it was information I should have known at least.

"You riding with me?" Sean asked.

I nodded and linked arms with him. "Yes, sir. Kieran's truck is too cramped to fit us."

"We could put people in the back," Kieran suggested.

Sean laughed. "Pass. Don't worry, I'll keep our girl safe."

Our girl...

Hearing him say that had all kinds of feelings spinning within my head and heart.

"You'd better," Kieran said.

Ever since the Arthur incident, they had been overly protective. Every morning Noah met me at my house and walked me to Tamara's before heading to school. I had to stop by the store to say hi to Sean to ensure he knew I was safe. Then the Gods met me at the school entrance.

After school I walked with Tamara, Noah, and Wade to Sean's store where we waited for him to clock out and go to Tamara's. Once football practice was over, the Gods picked me up and took me to Kieran's for our nightly workout sessions.

I wouldn't admit it to them, but it was nice to be stronger and not get winded as quickly.

After workouts, they drove me home, came inside, and sat on the couch to watch an episode of an old black and white cartoon Mama loved. We sat together in the living room laughing at the ridiculous cartoon characters, and then Mama shooed them out of the house.

It was already a routine and I loved it.

My weekends were split between the Gods and Geeks, as I was referring to them now.

They seemed fine with it and sometimes they even merged

their time with me so I could hang out with Kieran, Branson, Taylor, Noah, and Sean all at once.

Noah wasn't as keen on spending time with the Gods, but he said he would do whatever he had to to spend more time with me.

"Come on," Sean said, tugging on my arm. "Let's go."

"Yes, Guild Master," I said cheerfully.

He leaned close and whispered in my ear, "Hearing you say that has a completely different effect on me than when they say it. It might be better if you didn't call me that, except in private."

I turned my head and kissed his lips. "Yes, Guild Master."

He shivered and turned away from me. "Come on, let's hurry."

I chuckled, glad to know I had such an effect on him. A tool I could add to my arsenal for use at a later date.

Mike, Wade, and Noah were already there—papers, notebooks, pencils, and dice strewn around the large dining room table.

"Hey!" all three cheered when the five of us walked in.

"Our party hath grown in size!" Wade said in a strange accent.

"Oh, he gets to do an accent, but I can't?" Branson asked me.

I laughed. "You can do whatever accent you want, Branson."

He bowed, took my hand, and kissed the back of it. "Thank you, milady."

"Oy. Oy! No flirting with party members!" Mike said in an English accent.

We took seats, pulled out our papers and dice, and prepared.

I sat between Kieran and Noah and wasn't shocked when both took my hands in theirs.

How was I going to roll my dice?

Sean took a bit longer to set up and even put up a divider so we couldn't see his papers. He cleared his throat and said, "You are adventurers, just finished with an assignment; you sit inside a tavern to drink away the memories of your recent, bloody battle."

"Do we know each other?" Branson asked.

"He'll get there," Mike whispered.

"Aside from you seven, there are three barmaids, a dwarf with a battle axe that's chipped in several places, an old man with a cane sitting at the bar top drinking with shaky hands, and the bartender who is a sprite, younger man with a smile for anyone who comes in and a dagger for anyone who tries to leave without paying," Sean continued.

"Oh, this is going to be good," Wade said excitedly.

"What do you do?" Sean asked and leaned back, smiling.

"I raise my hand as the cutest barmaid walks by, stopping her," I say immediately.

Everyone stared at me.

Sean smirks. "She turns to you and asks, 'What can I get you, Lady Sira?'"

My eyes widened and then I narrowed them. "I draw my dagger and begin picking the dirt from beneath my fingernails with it. Then I ask, 'How do you know who I am, barmaid?'"

Sean's eyes go wide as he gets into the character of the barmaid. "'Oh, haven't you seen the posters?' the barmaid asks."

Before I can do more, Mike slams his hand on the table and leans forward. "Oy, where's me order?"

"Pipe down, I've got a hangover," Branson slurs and then pretends to hiccup.

I covered my mouth to keep from laughing. I knew he would totally get into the roleplaying part, but I hadn't realized he would go this far.

"You pipe down!" Taylor snapped. "Some of us are enjoying the scenery." He winked at me and then at Sean.

"The dwarf in the corner stands up, grabs his battle axe, and approaches your table, Lady Sira," Sean said.

"I cut in front of him and sit down opposite her," Kieran said quickly.

Always the protector.

"Excuse you? That seats taken," I said and folded my arms across my chest, pulling my hands out of Noah's and Kieran's.

"It is now," Kieran agreed with a nod.

"The dwarf hesitates, but then turns towards Lady Sira, drops to one knee and bows his head. 'My lady,' he says. 'I ask to join you on your quest.'"

"'I'm not on a quest at the moment,' I reply quickly," I said.

"The dwarf raises his head, looks at the barmaid, and then says, 'But the vampire king has put a bounty on your head. Are you not going to go to him and face him before the mercenaries and bounty hunters get you first?'"

"I say, 'Too late,'" Kieran said. "I draw my sword and put the tip at her throat. 'She is mine.'"

"I throw my mug at his head," Mike said, "and yell, 'Boo. I want to go on the adventure, too.'"

"Before anyone can react," Sean said. "The roof of the bar is torn off and a giant dragon roars above you all. Make your rolls for initiative. The time for battle is upon you all."

CHAPTER SIXTEEN

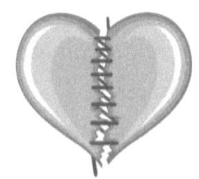

4 MONTHS LATER

"Merry Christmas!" Tamara shouted as she pushed open my front door.

Mom and I turned away from the tree we were putting the finishing touches on.

"Christmas isn't for two more days," I said, chuckling.

Tamara was followed by Noah, Wade, and Sean.

"It's Christmas all week," Tamara argued.

"She's just glad school is out for the break," Wade explained.

"That is definitely worth celebrating," I agreed.

"Would you all like some cocoa?" Mom asked.

"Yes, please!" all five of us said simultaneously.

"Ready for some small-town fun?" Wade asked.

"I'm up for whatever you guys want to do," I told them honestly.

"Awesome!" Wade cheered.

"You need warmer clothes," Noah said, eyeing me in my plaid pajama shirt and shorts.

"Come on, I'll help you dress appropriately," Tamara said, grabbed my hand, and dragged me up the stairs to my room. As soon as the door was shut behind us, she started prancing and squealing softly. "Guess what?"

"What?" I asked and pulled out my thick green winter dress that had a fur lined hood and attached mittens. It wasn't snowing here, but it was freezing.

"I think Mike is going to propose to me!" she squealed and then put her hands over her mouth.

My mouth dropped open. "What?"

"He came over last weekend and talked to my dad for over two hours. Afterwards, he wouldn't tell me what they discussed, but kept smiling and kissing my forehead. Then, today, Mama told me he is coming over on Christmas Day!" She squealed again before falling on her back onto my bed.

"But...you haven't even graduated yet," I whispered.

She rolled her eyes. "I'm eighteen already and there's no way I won't graduate. Besides, it's not like we'll get married right away."

"I'm so happy for you!" I shouted, fell on top of her on the bed, and hugged her.

"Have you finished your shopping?" she asked me and shoved me off of her.

"Yeah. I need to finish wrapping some of them, though," I admitted.

She sat up and looked around. "Does that mean my present is in here, unwrapped, ready for me to see early?"

I tossed a sock from the floor at her. "No! I wrapped yours first since you're a terrible sneak."

She pouted. "You're so mean to your best friend."

I yanked the dress on over my head, smoothed it down, and turned to face her. "How's this look?"

"Perfect! You should put some green eyeshadow on to match." She stood, grabbed my eyeshadow pallet and applied it for me before I could even decide. "Perfection! Now the boys will be the ones fighting to hide their drool."

I smacked her hip, both of us laughing.

"So, what do you think the guys are getting you?" Tamara asked me.

I groaned, stood, and brushed my hair one more time. "I wish I knew. I feel like my presents aren't going to be good enough and that they're going to get me something super cool and make me feel awful."

She rolled her eyes. "It's not like they are rich! They're just country boys all in love with one girl."

I blushed and turned my head away. "We're just friends."

"Right, you're all friends, but they aren't dating any other girls, don't spend time with any other girls, spend every second they can with you."

"Do you...think poorly of me?" I asked softly.

She hugged me. "No. I saw how things progressed and you didn't, and aren't, doing anything wrong. Had you been stringing them along, I would say something, but honestly, I feel more like they're stringing *you* along."

I shook my head. "It's not like that."

"Look, I'm not here to judge, but you really should think about your future. If you are still planning to leave, you need to bash it into their thick skulls to make them understand. Knowing them, they think they can convince you to stay here," she said softly.

She was right, but I didn't want to think about that. Especially not this week.

"Put on your thick socks and boots just in case it rains," she ordered me then left the room.

For the past few months, I'd let myself fall into the routine the guys had set and just enjoyed my time with them. It felt good to have friends and to have guys who were interested in me for more than my body or what I could give them. All they wanted was my time and attention.

In six months, that would change, though. In six months, we would graduate and I would be preparing for moving back to California. If we continued on our current path, our feelings would grow stronger, deeper, and it would be even harder for me to leave.

"Ready?" Sean asked from the stairs.

I glanced up, paused in my doorway, and swallowed hard.

He looked hot as sin; his glasses were gone tonight, his shirt was thick, but still showed off his broad shoulders, and his jeans were tight enough I'd caught Mama looking a time or two as he left.

His smile wilted and he walked up to me. "Cam, what's wrong?"

Dwelling on this now wouldn't do any of us any good. Tonight was not the night for dramatic decisions or revelations. Tonight, we would go have fun doing whatever it was these crazy southerners I loved did for the holidays.

I looked up and smiled wide. "Sorry, I'm ready. Let's go." I threaded our fingers together and brushed my lips across his. "Thank you for checking on me."

We hurried outside where the rest of the group waited for us.

Tamara looped her arm through mine and pulled me ahead of the guys. "You're sticking with me tonight. Those boys get alone time with you all the time. It's my turn, even though we aren't alone."

"We can start a girls' night," I said. "Paint our nails, gossip, vent about boys."

She smiled and nodded. "Let's do it! First and third Sunday nights?"

"Sounds perfect," I agreed.

"Why can't we come?" Wade asked with a pout.

"Because sometimes girls need time alone," Tamara said. "I haven't had a night without you all in years."

Wade pouted. "You don't like us anymore?"

"Ouch, Tamara. I didn't realize was were so annoying," Noah said and acted like he'd been hit in the chest by an arrow and pretended to tear it back out.

"And here I thought we were such good friends," Sean said with a sigh. "I think she's just mad that she missed out on our gaming sessions and had to hear about how fun they are from Mike."

"Mike won't shut up about how fun they are and insists on telling me everything that happened. I might as well have been there because I know everything," she said and rolled her eyes.

I chuckled and said, "You could come and just sit with Mike, not play."

"Nope, she'll distract him. Only players allowed," Noah said.

"Who made you king?" Tamara asked.

"Actually, there was this chick in a pond with a sword," I began and then paused.

Noah, Wade, and I burst into laughter at the inside joke from our recent gaming session.

She sighed. "Inside jokes. Lovely."

I hugged her arm. "So, what are we going to do tonight? You never told me."

My question was answered when the park came into view.

The streets were closed leading up to it; there were tents, vendors, and people dressed up in Dickens' style clothing.

"Oh, my gosh," I whispered. "A Dickens Faire?"

"I told you she would get it," Sean whispered to Noah.

"I don't have enough money," I said. "I should have asked Mama for more. I didn't know we'd be doing this."

"I'll spot you," Sean said with a smile.

With a squeal, I grabbed Tamara's hand and ran to the first vendor.

Jewelry, hair ornaments, leather bags and journals, food, drink, and so much more surrounded me.

I stood at the leather journal stand, looking at each one while biting my lip. They were gorgeous, but they were also pricey.

"Which is your favorite?" Noah asked me.

I shook my head. "They're too expensive."

He rolled his eyes. "I just asked which was your favorite."

"This one," I whispered and picked up a green journal with the Norse World Tree, Yggdrasill. Gently, I stroked the carved, raised edges of the tree.

"That is a pretty one," he agreed, picked up one with a dragon on it and held it up. "This is my favorite."

I smirked. "I'm not surprised you chose one with a dragon."

He shrugged. "I love dragons."

I put the journal back, moved to the next booth, and started gawking over the quill pens they had for sale. They had one out you could try writing with and I could barely write my own name legibly.

"You'll have to work on that penmanship," Tamara teased me.

I scoffed and held out the quill. "You try it."

Tamara took the quill, dipped it in the ink, and wrote her name in perfect cursive, even adding a few curly accents.

My jaw dropped.

She laughed. "Didn't I tell you that calligraphy was a favorite hobby of mine?"

"You've been holding out on me! I had no idea you could write so beautifully."

She shrugged and moved to the next vendor. "For school-work I just write as fast as I can. For fun, though, I like to draw things as beautifully as I can."

"Can you teach me?" I begged.

She laughed. "I can try, but your attempt looked like a two-year-old tried to write their name for the first time."

I elbowed her. "It wasn't that bad."

She shook her head while laughing even harder. "It so was. I should go back and ask for that piece of paper to show to the Gods. They might rethink your friendship."

I laughed and elbowed her again. "Rude!"

"Oh," she whispered and stopped at a set of trays with hair pins with little ornaments and jewels on the ends.

"Those are pretty," I whispered and picked up a silver one with an amethyst dangling from the end.

"What do you think?" Tamara asked, turning to show an extra-long one stuck through the hair she had twisted into a quick bun.

"The red goes great with your skin color," I said. "If you used red eyeshadow to tie it in, it would be perfect."

"What about the green?" she asked.

I sighed. "Every color looks great on you. You could pick any of these you wanted."

"It is three for fifteen dollars. Maybe I'll get three," she whispered, eyes focused on the trays, moving them around to find some with charms like a mermaid, sun, and unicorn.

I walked to the other side and browsed their earrings while I waited for her to make her selection.

"You don't wear earrings," Sean said. "Are they even pierced?"

I touched one of my earlobes. "They were pierced. I stopped wearing earrings at my last school."

"Why?" he asked softly and picked up a pair of silver studs.

"Because in a fight someone could grab a dangling earring and tear your ear open, which would severely distract you and could cause you to lose," I whispered.

He set the studs down, slid his hand from my chin up along my jaw until his fingers curled around my ear. "You could wear them now. No one is going to yank them out here."

Sylvia walked by with her cronies, all in gorgeous dresses, their hair curled, makeup done perfectly. She saw me, gave me a glare that could melt metal, and spun to go in the opposite direction.

"I don't know, I might still have one or two people who would pull out my earrings in a fight if they could," I whispered.

"Hey! Stop stealing her," Tamara said, grabbed my hand, and pulled me away from Sean.

Sean and I laughed, and I made sure to stick right by her side the rest of the night.

Wade and Noah brought us kettle corn and sodas.

We all sat on the grass and ate our snacks, watching the rest of the town milling about, purchasing things, eating, drinking, and ninety percent of them smiling.

"This is nice," I said softly. "Thank you for bringing me."

"You're welcome," Sean, Noah, Wade, and Tamara said at the same time.

We all laughed and then I rested my head on Tamara's shoulder. "Thank you for being my friend."

She wrapped her arm around my shoulders and squeezed. "Thank you for being mine."

"So, what's the plan for the rest of the night?" I asked.

"We have more vendors to see and then, they're going to start the show," she said.

"What show?" I asked.

They all looked at each other and then clamped their lips closed.

I sighed. "Fine, I'll wait to find out."

"There's my favorite girl," Branson said as he, Taylor, and Kieran walked over to us.

Tamara glared and tightened her hold on my shoulders. "No, shoo! She's mine tonight."

Kieran smirked. "Didn't know you swung that way, Tamara."

She rolled her eyes. "Shut up, K."

"We aren't trying to steal her away, promise," Taylor said and made an "X" on his chest. "We just wanted to say hi."

"Well, you did, now beat it," Tamara said and threw a piece of popcorn at Branson.

Branson caught it and popped it into his mouth. "Yum! Kettle corn! I haven't had that yet. Time to go!"

He waved and turned away. Taylor blew me a kiss. Kieran winked at me and then followed his friends.

We finished our snacks and continued walking around to the various vendors. I found a rose necklace that Mama would love, so I bought it and was ecstatic when they offered a box with a bow on top for free so I didn't even have to wrap it.

A bell started ringing and someone shouted something, but I couldn't hear or understand them.

Tamara grabbed my hand, her eyes wide and a huge smile on her face. "Come on! It's starting."

We went back to the grassy area we sat on before, but this time we stood.

Noah stood on my right and slipped his hand into mine, squeezing gently.

I squeezed his hand back and turned to smile up at him.

"You look beautiful," he whispered.

"Thank you," I said.

At the front of the crowd was a small wooden platform. The mayor, dressed in an old-style suit, walked up onto it, a scowl on his face. "We hear, there be witches amongst us!"

The crowd, mostly those dressed in the time-period clothing, gasped and began whispering to each other with wide eyes.

"Whom amongst us are the witches?" the mayor asked, put his hand over his eyes and looked out at the crowd. "Ah ha! I've spotted one. Tamara! You come up here and confess your witchy sins!"

Tamara squealed, released my hand, and jogged up to the front, the crowd parted to let her through.

"What is this?" I asked nervously.

"It's okay," Sean said as he came up to my other side. "It's just an act."

"They pick a few people out from the crowd to participate," Noah whispered and squeezed my hands. "It's okay."

"I confess I am a witch!" Tamara said once she got to the podium. She spun, raised her hands in the air, and fireworks shot up into the sky behind the platform.

The crowd, including me, gasped.

"Name your accomplices!" the mayor shouted.

"There be a warlock amongst us!" Tamara said.

"A warlock?" the mayor gasped. "Whomst could it be?"

"Kieran!" she shouted and pointed to the right side of the crowd.

Everyone's head swiveled to the side where the Gods stood.

Kieran smirked, stalked up to the platform, spun around dramatically and said, "I am not a warlock! I am a god!"

The crowd laughed, but then fireworks exploded in a multitude of colors high up into the sky.

Kids cheered, and my mouth dropped open.

What kind of town was this?

"Are there more amongst the crowd?" the mayor asked. "Are there more witches and warlocks living amongst us?"

Kieran looked at me, and I shook my head. He smiled. "There's a goddess amongst us."

"A goddess?" the mayor's wife, dressed in a dress with a hoop skirt that stuck out at least two feet around her. "Whomst is this goddess? Is she one to worship or fear?"

"Both," he said.

"Point her out! Let us bring her here to start this celebration of the winter solstice!" the mayor shouted.

"Cameron," he said.

I knew he was going to say me and yet when my name came out of his mouth, I froze and felt uncertain I had heard correctly.

Sean pushed me forward and then the crowd parted so I had a clear path up to him and Tamara.

He was going to die for this.

Falling back on my false bravado I'd used many times before, I straightened my spine and walked confidently up to Kieran.

He bowed, took my hand, and kissed the back of it. "Goddess."

Tamara curtsied. "Goddess."

Oh, I was going to murder her, too!

I turned and the explosion of the fireworks didn't make me

jump. The crowd staring at me didn't make me nervous. Sylvia and her cronies glaring at me, in addition to several other girls from the high school, had me swallowing thickly.

"Shall we begin?" the mayor asked me.

I nodded. "Let the Solstice begin."

He smiled, threw his hands into the air, and said, "Let the Solstice begin!"

Kieran took my hand, turned us around so I stood between him and Tamara, and we watched the fireworks show together.

"You're so dead," I whispered to him.

He squeezed my hand. "Yet you're still holding my hand."

"Mine's cold," I lied.

He chuckled. "Whatever you say, Goddess."

"Were you in on this plan?" I asked Tamara.

She shrugged. "I'm a sucker for corny cuteness. He told me what he wanted to do and I agreed. Plus, the mayor thought it was great that we wanted to include you."

"Hmph," I replied, watching as a firework shot high into the air and blossomed into a flower.

"You're beautiful," Kieran said. "Tonight, though, you truly look like a goddess."

My cheeks warmed at the compliment. "Thank you."

"Are we still okay to come over for dinner tomorrow?" he asked.

I nodded. "Mama is excited. She likes cooking for a lot of people and hasn't been able to since we moved and aren't near any of her family."

"You'll have to wrap the rest of the presents tonight," Tamara reminded me.

I groaned. "Yeah, I know!"

"I could help you wrap them," Kieran offered.

"No!" I said quickly.

He arched a brow.

"I have to wrap yours," I whispered and looked back at the fireworks. The next one was a red smiley face.

"We told you that you didn't have to get us anything," he whispered.

I looked over at him. "Did you get me something?"

He didn't respond.

"Exactly," I said and looked back at the fireworks.

He chuckled softly, took his hand from mine, and slipped his arm around my waist. "Feisty tonight, aren't we?"

"Only because two of my friends plotted against me," I whispered.

"Not two of them," Sean said behind me.

I spun, mouth open. "You were all in on this?"

Wade and Noah nodded

"Us, too!" Taylor and Branson said as they joined us.

Standing surrounded by my friends as fireworks brightened the sky overhead, I realized that this was what I had craved most of my childhood. A group of friends who all got along, that I could spend time with, and didn't have to worry about them stabbing me in the back. Literally and figuratively.

Tears sprang to my eyes, and I pulled my hood on to hide my face as I sniffled. "I love you guys."

Tamara hugged me and then there was a massive pressure as the entire group, Gods and Geeks, had a huge hug puddle.

"We love you, too," Tamara said and pushed my hood back to wipe my cheeks. "You've brightened our lives in a way that we hadn't realized was possible. We didn't realize there was a chunk of darkness around us until you came and lit it up."

I sniffled, but more tears came anyway. Throwing my arms around her neck, she wrapped her arms around my waist and cried into my shoulder.

"Oh, man," Branson said and sniffled. "You're going to make me cry, too."

"How is a big man like you such a crybaby?" Wade asked with a chuckle.

"It's called being in touch with my feelings. Toxic masculinity has no power over me," he said and blew his nose loudly.

"Can we go back to hugging?" Wade asked. "That was nice."

Everyone laughed, but then gathered together for another group hug.

CHAPTER SEVENTEEN

"Stop fussing with your dress," Mama chastised me. "Everything is set and ready."

"I'm sorry. This is just the first time I've had friends over for dinner on Christmas Eve," I reminded her. "I want it to be perfect."

She waggled her brows. "You sure it's not because those Gods are coming?"

I sighed. "Mama, stop calling them that."

She giggled as she pulled biscuits out of the oven. "If I were your age I'd be going after them, too."

"Oh, which one of us would you hunt?" Branson asked as he, Taylor, Kieran, Sean, Noah, Wade, and Tamara walked inside.

"Merry Christmas!" Tamara yelled and raced across the living room to hug me.

I hugged her tightly. "Merry Christmas."

She looked at the tree. "Can I put presents under there?"

I nodded.

Kieran carried a huge red bag over, opened it, and started taking presents out.

My mouth dropped. "Uh, what are all of those?"

"Presents," he said with a smirk.

Sean snapped a picture of me and chuckled. "You were right, her expression was priceless."

"Huh?" I asked, looking from Sean to Kieran.

"He said you would freak out if he brought in a bag of presents and he was right. So, we put all of our presents in the bag," Sean explained.

I smacked his arm and then Kieran's playfully. "Butts."

"I've got hot apple cider and hot cocoa on the stove," Mama said. "Who wants what?"

"Cocoa!" Sean called out.

"Cider, please," Kieran said while he continued pulling presents from the bag.

Mama took everyone's orders and returned to the kitchen. Taylor and Wade followed her in to help her.

Noah dropped down beside Kieran and helped him take out the presents and put them around the base of the tree.

Sean took my hand and tugged me over to the couch so I could sit between him and Tamara.

Tamara touched the sleeve of my emerald dress. "This is beautiful."

"Thanks," I said and stroked the fur of her Santa-style dress. "This is super festive and cute."

She fluffed her collar. "I made it myself."

My mouth dropped a second time. "No way!"

"You don't know how to sew?" she asked.

Mama scoffed. "Only ask her to sew something if you want it covered in her blood from poking her fingers constantly."

I glared. "It's not my fault I suck at doing girly things."

"You are hopeless," Tamara said with a sigh.

"She's really good at math," Noah said.

Mama looked at him. "You checking her grades for me?"

He laughed and shook his head. "During our games you have to add several numbers together at once and she does it faster than the rest of us."

Mama looked at me. "Huh, guess you got that from your father."

"You're good at math, too," I said.

She shrugged. "I can be. So, are you guys hungry?"

"Starving!" Wade said.

She beamed. "Great! Let's go sit at the table and start eating."

We all walked to the table, Mama and I sat at the ends, and the rest took seats along the sides.

The dinner was the liveliest ever to happen in our house and halfway through it, Mama started crying while smiling.

"You okay?" Sean asked and set his hand on top of hers.

She nodded and wiped her tears with her napkin. "I'm just so happy to see so many smiling faces at my dinner table." She looked at me. "Especially yours."

Tears built, but I blinked them away. "No! No crying on Christmas, remember?"

She chuckled. "But good tears are different." She stood and said, "I'll be right back. I'm going to grab something."

I worried about her, but she was smiling as she left, even when she turned away from the table, so it didn't seem like she was going off to cry alone.

My suspicion was confirmed when she returned not even a minute later, an envelope in her hand.

"Here," she said and held it out to me.

Frowning, I took it. It only had my name on it in her handwriting. "What is it?"

She beamed. "Your Christmas present, well, one of them."

"I can wait," I insisted, but she shook her head.

"I want you to open this in front of your friends. I'm sure they'll be excited," she said.

Nerves made my hands shake as I opened it, promptly earning me a paper cut.

"Ouch," I hissed and stuck the finger in my mouth. I finally got the envelope open and pulled out the piece of paper.

I leapt upright, knocked my chair over, and threw my arms around her neck while squealing.

"What is it?" Tamara asked and snatched the paper from my hand.

"You're the best Mama ever!" I screamed.

She patted my back. "I thought you'd like it."

"A certificate for a tattoo!" Tamara yelled. "Lucky."

"Oh!" Sean said with a wide smile. "You're finally going to join the inked club."

"What are you going to get?" Kieran asked.

My smile wilted slightly, but I didn't want to ruin the mood by explaining my tattoo, so I said. "You'll have to wait and see."

"Tease!" Taylor accused.

"You've got an appointment for the twenty-seventh," Mama said. "I went to the shop and did a lot of questioning before I agreed to let you do it and signed the papers already to give you permission. Since this is such a small town and all, you don't have to take me with you."

"I love you!" I shouted and hugged her again.

She laughed and hugged me back. "Love you too, Cameron."

Dinner was finished, so we cleaned up the table and then gathered in the living room.

My nerves were even higher now as I prepared to have the presents I had purchased for everyone opened. What if they hated what I chose? I had put a lot of time and thought into the presents, but that didn't mean that I hadn't gotten them wrong.

"Alright, I nominate Branson to play Santa," Mama said and sat in her reclining chair with a steaming cup of cider in her hand.

"Yes, Ma'am!" Branson said, sat down cross-legged by the tree, and started sorting the presents into piles. "Do you want everyone to get one or do you make people open them one at a time so we get stared at?"

Mama laughed. "Well, I can tell which one you prefer, so I'll let you make the decision."

He smiled wide and then tossed everyone a present. Once we all had one, he said, "Open!"

The present in my lap was from Tamara. I opened it and pulled out the hair stick with the amethyst jewel on it.

"Thank you!" I gasped and immediately put it in my hair.

She opened the present in her lap, mine, and gaped at the signed paperback from her most recently favorite author. She screamed and jumped over Taylor to hug me. "What? How?"

I smirked. "I've been part of her fan group for a few years and every year she does a signed paperback order. So, I ordered it for you."

Tamara opened it and read the personalized note inside, her eyes welling with tears. "Thank you."

"Oh, great, now my present is going to suck," Wade groaned.

"Any present is a good present," Tamara assured him and nudged his shoulder with hers.

"Next!" Branson said and started passing out presents again.

Mama got my present, her eyes widening.

I got a present from Taylor, but when he saw, he snatched the box back. "No, you can't open mine yet."

"Oh, right. Sorry," Branson apologized and tossed me a different present.

I scowled at them. "What? Rude."

"You have to open his last," Branson said and shrugged.

"It's okay, you'll like mine," Sean said with a big smile.

I returned his smile. "I'm sure I will."

"Okay, go!" Branson said.

The sound of tearing paper and gasps of delight filled the air.

Sean's present was a boxed set of his favorite author's most popular series.

"Thank you!" I told him. "Now I can read them."

"I was planning a re-read, so I thought we could read them together," he said.

My heart warmed. "I'd like that."

"Cameron, this is beautiful," Mama said.

"Want me to help you put it on?" Kieran asked and stood.

He helped her put the necklace on and she stroked the rose.

"I'm glad you like it," I said.

Branson passed out the next set of presents.

This time, I got Noah's and he got mine.

His present was a little heavy.

"Open!" Branson said.

I opened the present carefully, gasping when I saw the leather Yggdrasill journal. "You didn't!"

He pulled out the dice set I'd purchased that was painted in galaxy colors.

"These are gorgeous," he said and rolled one in his hand before rolling it on the table.

I hugged him. "Thank you."

He hugged me back. "Thank you! These are going to make a world of difference when we play. My other set was chipped."

That was exactly why I'd purchased it for him.

We went through the next gifts until I finally got Taylor's. I hadn't received one from Kieran, but I didn't want to bring it up. I wasn't sure if it was a money issue or what and I didn't want to make him feel bad. I truly didn't care. I loved that he was here at all.

"Okay," Taylor said. "You can open it now."

Everyone stood up and put their shoes on, despite them still having gifts to open.

"You are all being suspicious," I whispered.

"Open it. Open it," Branson chanted while putting his shoes on.

Pulling off the lid of the box, I found a keyring. I looked at them and back at the keyring.

"Come on," Taylor said and held out his hand.

I stood, keyring in hand, and let him lead me outside.

Mama was smiling, and I glared. "You're in on this?"

She nodded. "They asked my approval first."

What could it be? It was something Mama approved of, so it wasn't a car or house or anything.

"Close your eyes," Taylor instructed me.

Branson put his hands over my eyes. "No peeking."

I stumbled a bit as we went down the stairs, but Branson and Taylor steadied me.

"Ready?" Taylor asked.

I nodded. "Yes."

Branson removed his hands, and I opened my eyes.

Before us sat a shiny, purple dirt bike with a matching purple helmet.

I gasped, looked at Taylor, the dirt bike, and back to Taylor. "Wha—"

He chuckled. "This is all yours, Cammy."

I threw my hands around his neck and kissed his cheek. "Thank you!"

"It's too late to take it for a ride, plus that motor is too loud and will disturb the neighbors," Mama said. "You can ride it tomorrow. Back in the house."

"Can I sit on it at least?" I begged.

"Two minutes," she said. "I'm going back inside. It's too cold out here." She wrapped her arms around herself and hurried inside.

"I'm going in, too," Tamara said. "The bike is pretty."

Wade, Sean, and Noah went inside as well, leaving me alone with the Gods.

I threw my leg over the bike and sat on it, setting my hands on the handlebars.

My own dirt bike! I could drive this around town if I wanted to or go for rides with the guys. Though, it was sad that I wouldn't be able to ride behind one of them anymore.

A camera flashed.

"What?" I asked, turning to look at the offending phone and phone owner.

Taylor smiled. "You were smiling and it was the perfect photo op."

"Send it to me!" Branson said.

"Me, too," Kieran said.

"We better get back inside," I said and climbed back off the back, petting it as I walked around it.

"Wait, there's one more thing we have to give you," Kieran said.

"If you got me one of those kid's bike's horns, you can't get mad when I honk it all the time," I said with a smirk.

"Well, now I know what to get you for your birthday," Taylor teased.

The three of them stood side by side, facing me, and then

in unison dropped to one knee while Kieran pulled out a ring box.

My eyes opened so wide I worried they would get stuck like that.

"Will you accept this promise ring, from us?" Kieran asked.

"What am I promising?" I asked breathlessly.

"That you'll stay with all of us," Branson said.

"I'm moving back to California when I turn eighteen, remember?" I asked softly.

They all nodded.

"We plan to go with you," Kieran said. "Wherever you go, that's where we'll go. You're our world and we don't want to live in a town where we won't see your beautiful face every day."

The desire to scream yes was there, but so was the desire to ask about Sean and Noah.

"Are you asking me to be exclusive to you three?" I asked softly.

"Sean and Noah know about this. They agreed we could ask you and we agreed that if you decided to continue dating them that we would be fine with that, too, but only with them. We want you to be exclusive with us five," Taylor said.

"You could have any girl you want. You could go into the middle of the town, yell out that you want someone for a night, and they'd line up. Why would you consider sharing one girl with four other guys?"

Why was my stupid mouth asking questions like this? I should have accepted it and moved on.

"We love you," Kieran said, stood, and walked to me. He set his hand on my cheek and said, "I love you, Lavender."

"We all love you," Noah said behind Kieran.

Kieran turned sideways so I could see behind him.

Sean and Noah stood beside Taylor and Branson.

"You're okay with this?" I asked.

They both nodded.

Sean smiled. "None of us are worthy of keeping you to ourselves."

"And I would rather share you with friends than lose you," Noah said softly.

I took the ring box out of Kieran's hand and bit my lip. They were serious? This was a dream, wasn't it? I would wake up with a naked finger in the morning and be sad. I just knew it.

Kieran took the ring out and put it on my right ring finger.

"I love you all, too," I whispered.

EPILOGUE

Hiding the relationships from Mama was hard, but we made it through the school year without her knowing. One month after finishing school, we packed up the trucks and said goodbye to our small town, Mama, and Tamara.

Saying goodbye to Tamara was the hardest, but we promised to keep in touch. Plus, we would be coming back in six months for her wedding.

The trip took four days to make, but when we pulled up to the three-story log cabin my father had left me in his will, it was all worth it.

"Welcome to our new home," I said proudly and skipped up to the front door, unlocking it.

"This place is huge!" Branson exclaimed.

Noah swept me off my feet, holding me in his arms before I could walk in. "You're supposed to be carried over the threshold."

I giggled. "That's when you get married."

"Well, since our country doesn't allow that, you'll just have to pretend," he said.

He walked in, set me down, and then kissed me deeply.

"How large is the plot of land?" Taylor asked.

"Ten acres," I called out to him, making my way down the hallway to explore all of the rooms.

Mama had shown me pictures of the house and told me that Dad had paid for a groundskeeper in advance to ensure the house didn't fall into disrepair before I was old enough to move in.

We were in the woods, but a big city was only half an hour away, which would make it easier for everyone to find jobs.

I found a job at the nearby veterinarian's office, so I could get some experience as a receptionist. Working there would help pay the bills so I would be able to get through all the schooling necessary to become a veterinary technician and then, eventually, a veterinarian myself at that same office.

"Ten acres means plenty of land to create our dirt bike track," Kieran said.

I nodded. "There's also a shop about an acre behind the house so we can store the bikes there and you can work on them in it when needed."

"To the shop!" Taylor shouted.

Sean slipped his arm around my waist and tugged me close to his side. "It's perfect for us."

I nodded. "It is."

"You're perfect," he whispered and kissed me softly.

"Pretty sure you're the perfect ones," I chuckled. I twirled my hair which was back to its normal color since I had run out of dye.

"It's okay, you'll always be our purple girl," Sean said and tugged on my hair. "Forever."

ABOUT THE AUTHOR

Daisy Emory is the contemporary romance and contemporary reverse harem romance pseudonym for USA Today Bestselling Author Catherine Banks.

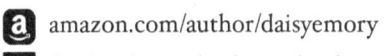 amazon.com/author/daisyemory
facebook.com/catherinebanksauthor

ABOUT THE AUTHOR

Catherine Banks is a USA Today bestselling fantasy author who writes in several fantasy subgenres and has multiple pseudonyms. She began writing fiction at only four years old and finished her first full-length novel at the age of fifteen. She is married to her soulmate and best friend, Avery, who she has two amazing children with. After her full-time job, she reads books, plays video games, and watches anime shows and movies with her family to relax. Although she has lived in Northern California her entire life, she dreams of traveling around the world. Catherine is also C.E.O. of Turbo Kitten Industries™, a company with many hats including being a book publisher and Etsy store full of nerdy fun.

facebook.com/catherinebanksauthor

twitter.com/catherineebanks

amazon.com/author/catherinebanks

bookbub.com/authors/catherine-banks

MORE FROM DAISY EMORY

The Boyfriend Deal

Their Purple Girl

ACCIDENTAL MOBSTER SERIES
Accidental Mobster
Unintentional Pirate*

*Coming Soon

CHILDREN'S BOOKS
Calvin's Alien Adventure

YOUNG ADULT PARANORMAL & FANTASY ROMANCE SERIES
Artemis Lupine Series
Song of the Moon
Kiss of a Star
Healed by the Fire
Battles of the Night
Artemis Lupine, The Complete Series

Little Death Bringer Duology
Mercenary
Protector
Little Death Bringer, The Official Coloring Book

Pirate Princess Series
Pirate Princess
Princess Triumvirate

ADULT PARANORMAL & FANTASY ROMANCE SERIES

Zodiac Shifters Paranormal Romance Series

Centaur's Prize

Tiger Tears

Lion About

Ciara Steele Novella Series

True Faces

Barbaric Tendencies

ADULT REVERSE HAREM PARANORMAL & FANTASY ROMANCE SERIES

Her Royal Harem Series

Royally Entangled

Royally Exposed

Royally Elected

Royally Enraged

Her Royal Harem, The Complete Series

The Demon's Fair

Her Royal Harem, The Coloring Book

Wings of Vengeance Series

Of Dragons and Cruelty

Of Minotaurs and Sacrifice

Wings of Vengeance, The Complete Series

Anderelle: Minloa Trilogy

Queen of the Stars

Empress of the Galaxy

Goddess of the Universe

Anderelle: Minloa, The Complete Series

Bonds of Madness Series

Sealing the Deal

Her Super Harem Series

Lucky Strike

Pandamonium*

*Coming Soon

MORE FROM CATHERINE BANKS

STANDALONE YOUNG ADULT PARANORMAL & FANTASY ROMANCE BOOKS

Monster Academy

Daughter of Lions

Lady Serra and the Draconian

Of Sky and Sea

The Last Werewolf

Sybil Deceived

STANDALONE YOUNG ADULT PARANORMAL & FANTASY REVERSE HAREM ROMANCE BOOKS

Moon Academy

STANDALONE ADULT PARANORMAL & FANTASY ROMANCE BOOKS

Demonic Contract

Anja's Secret

Dragon's Blood

Last Ama Princess

Transforming Rose

Alys of Asgard
Phoenix Possessed
Stone Heart

STANDALONE URBAN FANTASY BOOKS
The Pawn

www.ingramcontent.com/pod-product-compliance
Lightning Source LLC
Chambersburg PA
CBHW021239260626
47155CB00004BA/1222